40 and (So Over) Fixing It

SILVER FOXES OF BLACK WOLF'S BLUFF 3

ELLA SHERIDAN

Praise for Silver Foxes of Black Wolf's Bluff

"[A] fascinating series."

WENDY'S BOOK BLOG

"Fun, easy to read, and the start of what seems to be a dynamite series."

THE ORIGINAL MRS. P

"Loved the town and omg that passion between JD and Lily burned the pages!!! Amazing book!"

CK BOOKSTAMMER

"Where sexual tension and drama really heats up in the kitchen."

THE DRAGON DEN BOOK BLOG

"Going back to Black Wolf's Bluff … was such a delight."

GERI'S BOOKISH LIFE

Also by Ella Sheridan

Silver Foxes of Black Wolf's Bluff
40 and (Tired of) Faking It
40 and (No Longer) Fighting It
40 and (*So* Over) Fixing It

Assassins
Assassin's Mark
Assassin's Prey
Assassin's Heart
Assassin's Game

Southern Nights
Teach Me
Trust Me
Take Me

Southern Nights: Enigma
Come for Me
Deceive Me
Destroy Me
Deny Me
Desire Me

Archai Warriors
Griffin Undone
Phoenix Falling

If Only

Only for the Weekend

Only for the Night

Only for the Moment

Only If You Stay

Secrets

Unavailable

Undisclosed

Unshakable

For news on Ella's new releases, free book opportunities, and more, sign up for her monthly newsletter at ellasheridanauthor.com.

Join Ella's Escape Room on Facebook for daily fun, games, and first dibs on all the news!

To Erin. Your time has come.

Acknowledgments

This book would not have been completed if not for the encouragement of my first reader, Linda. Thank you, my friend. Your love for my books and your friendship with me are special gifts I will always cherish.

To my critique partners, Gina and Nina. (Yes, they rhyme!) Y'all talked me through so many issues with this book. I can't thank you enough for your support and, maybe most of all, patience!

Thank you to Eric and Christian and Jaycee for this amazing cover. Christian, you make the perfect Carter.

My life is also made richer by the love and support of my family and friends. Thank you to Dani, Hannah, Tammy, Cindi, Kelly, Angi, my kids, and my phenomenal assistant, Alyssa, who helps keep me sane. (I'm sure I'm also forgetting people!) I couldn't make it without you all. Love you!

CHAPTER
One

C arter Deveraux was going to kill his sister. No more blind dates, no more harassing him till he agreed. He wouldn't have to put up with Emma's pestering because she wouldn't be around to pester him anymore. He would make sure of it.

"Carter?"

The woman standing beside his table had to be at least half his age. Maybe more, given he would be fifty in a few months and she didn't look like she was out of her teens. That might just be the clothes, though; the barely knee-length plaid skirt she wore was more suited to a Catholic schoolgirl than a dinner at a restaurant listed in the top ten of New York City. Come to think of it, so was the tight white button-down. And God almighty, she was wearing knee socks.

Thank God he hadn't taken her to the Prime—Linc would never let him hear the end of this.

He belatedly realized he was still sitting and came to his feet. "Chloe?" Was that the name Emma had given him? Or maybe it was Zoey? All the women she'd set him up with were starting to run together at this point, which probably meant he should take a long, long break from dating.

1

As he pulled out the woman's chair, trying hard not to stare down the deep vee of her open shirt, he amended that thought. A permanent break would be best, at least if it was Emma engineering the dates.

"Zoey." She smiled up at him, her lips a soft pink that reminded him of his cousin's youngest daughter. He tried hard to shake that thought as he returned to his seat.

"I apologize, Zoey. It's nice to meet you."

Their waiter came by with the bottle of Screaming Eagle Sauvignon Blanc he'd ordered before Zoey arrived, and Carter resisted the urge to card his own date to verify her age.

And he'd thought having a ten-year-old son made him feel old. He couldn't resist rubbing a hand over the beard that covered his jaw—a beard that was more white than dark blond these days—as he stared down at the menu. Emma had to have set him up with Zoey just to mess with him. This wasn't about making up for Carter being alone while Thad was with his mother for the weekend. This was about Emma fucking with her older brother, and when he finally escaped this nightmare of a date, he was going straight to wherever his sister was and strangling her.

After they ordered, Carter poured Zoey a glass of the wine, sticking to water himself. "Where did you say you knew Emma from?" His sister seemed to know everyone and made friends as easily as other people breathed.

Zoey fingered a strand of her silky blonde hair, which he had to admit was eye-catching as it fell over her shoulders. "We met at Zen."

Of course they had. Emma's favorite bar, right around the corner from her apartment. Sometimes he thought she spent more time there than she did at home. Of course, she didn't cook, so Zen's above-average kitchen made meals convenient. And everyone loved her there. Literally the entire bar lit up when she came in.

That was his sister for you. Life of the party—and the source of trouble, always.

"Oh. When was that?"

"Last week."

As Zoey told the story of meeting a group of friends at the bar, then striking up a conversation with Emma over martinis, he resisted the urge to lecture her on the dangers of trusting people in the city, particularly on dates. He wasn't her parent, after all.

Not that she seemed bothered by their age difference. She was currently fingering her wineglass as she stared up at him adoringly. That look had him shifting uncomfortably in his seat.

"So…you're a daddy."

He narrowed his eyes. "I'm a father, yes."

She traced the soft curve of her glass, the long pink tip of her fingernail matching that baby-pink lipstick. "Do you believe in corporal punishment?"

He choked on the swallow of water he'd taken just to give himself something to do with his hands. "Do I what?"

She glanced up at him from beneath unnaturally long lashes that framed soft, innocent-looking blue eyes. "You know…spanking."

His lips tightened. He really was going to strangle Emma. "No. No, I don't spank my boy."

"Boy?" Zoey straightened in her seat, the flirtatious facade falling away in favor of a confused pout. "You have boys?"

"I have a son." Surely Emma had told her. Oh, not details about Thaddeus, of course, but that he had a child.

She tilted her head, and a lock of golden hair curved over one side of her face. "But have you ever wanted a baby girl?"

"Sure, maybe." Although he was getting a bit old for that. His ex, Rachel, hadn't wanted children until her career had been well-established. She'd also been ten years younger than him. Bringing home a newborn was a totally different thing at thirty than at forty. He was definitely feeling his age with Thad rapidly approaching his teen years.

At least his son hadn't decided he was too old to cuddle with his old man yet.

"How about now?"

His gaze jerked from the cut-crystal glass he held to the woman across the table from him. What the hell was she talking about? "Now?"

"Yeah." She smiled, the flirtatious curve of her lips dotted perfectly in the center with a drop of her wine. He watched in horrified fascination as her tongue sneaked out and swiped up the last lingering bit. "Now. There are plenty of baby girls available if you just…look around."

Baby girl.

Daddy.

Baby girl.

Daddy.

Spanking.

"No." The word shot from his mouth with zero finesse. "No, definitely not now. Not—"

Zoey's flirtatious look shattered, laughter taking over. "I'm sorry, I can't—"

He couldn't stop staring as Zoey leaned back in her chair, clutching her stomach as if it ached as she laughed and laughed. Each time the sound eased off, she'd take another look at him and off she went again. He was beginning to get irritated when she finally caught her breath enough to explain.

"I'm sorry, Carter." Chuckles bubbled up, interrupting her words. "I thought I could do this, but I just can't keep it together. The look on your face…"

More laughter. What was wrong with his face?

And then he remembered.

"She put you up to this, didn't she?" he asked sourly. He'd even considered the idea earlier. The Catholic schoolgirl outfit

4

—and that's definitely what it was, he could see now—had tipped him off, but he'd never considered Zoey being in on it.

And thank God she was. Saved him from some very awkward conversation after the baby-girl comment.

He ran a hand down his face, scrubbing hard. Now that he thought about it, strangling might be too good for Emma.

When he looked again, Zoey was still struggling to control her amusement. Her laughter made him feel about the same age as Methuselah.

"She did put me up to it," Zoey confirmed. Her bright smile dimmed a bit as she watched him. "You don't mind, do you?"

His chuckle was still a bit reluctant. "You, I don't mind. Emma…"

"She's in for it later, I gather?"

"Definitely." From the corner of his eye he noticed their waiter approaching with full plates of food and sighed, releasing his pent-up irritation at his sister—for now. "But that doesn't mean we can't enjoy dinner."

And they did. When Zoey dropped the flirtatious facade, he found a pleasant young woman—still far too young for him at twenty-four—who was easy to talk to and spend time with. She told him how she'd met Emma during a "munch" her BDSM group was having at Zen, how Emma had overheard a bit of conversation and introduced herself. Which didn't surprise him at all. And the sense of fun he got from Zoey told him exactly why she'd agreed to this blind date.

"Besides"—Zoey shrugged as they lingered a bit, waiting for dessert—"you never know when an older guy is going to be interested in someone a bit younger."

"I don't think it's difficult to find an older man who'll go for a younger woman." That seemed to be the preferred scenario with too many men he knew.

"But not you, huh?"

"My son is nearly half your age, Zoey," he told her.

ELLA SHERIDAN

Her laughter said she didn't take offense. "Well, I'm sorry to hear that."

After dinner, he hailed a taxi in the early evening rush of traffic, settled Zoey inside, and prepaid the fare before giving her a wave as she drove away, all the while thinking about how many times in the past year he'd sent a woman home in a taxi, either after dinner or after something else. He wasn't celibate and he had no objections to a little fun, but women didn't stay overnight on the rare occasions Thad was with his mother and Carter found someone he was interested in. After this, though, he felt like a moratorium on dating was a necessity to cleanse his palate.

A daddy?

As he waited at the corner for the light to change, he snatched his phone from his back pocket, then crossed the street with the crowd, beginning the ten-block walk to his penthouse. His temples tightened with a headache as he clicked on his sister's name and waited. Emma picked up just as he came to the next cross street.

She was already laughing.

"I guess you thought that was funny."

"I don't even have to hear your version of what happened to know it was damn hilarious," Emma said, her laughter nearly choking her. She always reminded him of sunshine, which allowed her to get away with far more little-sister shit than he would like to admit. Today, though, he'd forgotten his sunglasses and wasn't in the mood.

"Putting Zoey in that position wasn't funny."

Emma's laughter didn't dim the least bit. "She was in on the whole thing. How'd you like the outfit, by the way?"

He growled.

Emma snickered. "Lighten up, *Daddy*."

"If you'd like I can come over there and show you what corporal punishment is all about."

6

"Don't think so," Emma sing-songed. "Even our daddy couldn't get away with that."

Not that he'd tried much. Emma was a force of nature, bowling all of them over. When she got her head wrapped around an idea, there was no shaking it. Unfortunately his dating life was the idea she'd wrapped around, and she wasn't letting loose.

He had to stop appeasing her.

"Tell me you didn't have a little fun," she said. "You could be at home in that New York loft, looking out on a bustling city with silence behind you. With Thad at his mom's…"

"It's quiet. I know." He sighed, releasing his irritation with his breath. "I actually do like quiet every once in a while."

"You'd wallow in it if I let you."

"At least next week I'll be gone and you won't be able to throw any new prospects at me." He and Thad were headed to the Tennessee mountains to see JD and his new fiancée. Apparently the mansion was surrounded by woods that would be perfect for Thad to get out and explore. Even if the idea of woods gave Carter hives. Talk about quiet. He definitely wasn't a woods kind of guy. He wasn't sure why JD seemed to enjoy it so much. Or Lincoln, who thrived on the adrenaline of his constantly packed Manhattan restaurant.

Guess sex could addle any man's brains.

"Watch it or I'll follow you down there," Emma warned.

He shut up and let her babble on about meeting Zoey, which led to various other topics in a stream of consciousness he could barely follow. Yes, he was definitely looking forward to getting away next week. He loved his family, but their mission to make sure he was happy since his divorce was getting a little too intrusive.

Especially Emma. Maybe he'd get lucky and his cell phone wouldn't get reception at JD's place.

Emma was winding down about the time he reached the

7

door to his building. "I'm about to hit the elevator, Sis. I'll have to catch you later."

"You better. I plan to get all the juicy tidbits from Zoey in the meantime. Bye!"

Carter groaned. Of course she would. And every last moment would be dissected until she found just the right pieces to rib him about.

Great.

When was he leaving?

CHAPTER

Two

E rin clutched the collar of her coat closed against the chill wind sweeping through the valley, and glared down at the arrogant male blocking her exit at the bottom of her front-porch steps.

"Willard!" She stomped her booted foot. "Go away! I've told you, I'm not interested in you."

Willard stared up at her, blinking his beady bird eyes, his gorgeous display of turquoise and yellow and purple peacock feathers spread high into the air. At her words—or maybe it was her tone—he shook the feathers and began a slow turn, circling to show off his beautiful plumage.

"Yes," Erin admitted, "you're stunning. Okay? Now go away."

Willard blinked up at her again and gave a chirp. Took one, two, three steps toward her stairs. Another chirp as he tilted his head, almost as if asking her a question. Probably wondering when she was going to give in and agree that she was his mate, different species aside.

As if.

With a heavy sigh she glanced at her watch and realized she was now officially three minutes late to meet Lily for lunch at Casa Blanca. A frantic search told her there was no help in sight; her in-laws were probably inside eating their own lunch at the moment, completely unaware that the wayward head of their peacock brood had gone a-courtin'.

"Willard…" The bird's name came out a whine. "I just wanna go to lunch."

Giving up on getting him to move, she backed her way toward the front door and inside the house. As she watched through the cut-out panes of glass, Willard came up the stairs and began to strut back and forth across her long farmhouse porch.

Perfect.

Digging her keys out of her purse, she made her hasty way through the house toward the side door. Sneaking past a stupid bird wasn't something she really wanted to admit to other people, but she didn't have time to waste and Willard wasn't responding to logic. Carefully pushing the door open to avoid that tell-tale squeak if the hinges were forced too fast, she eased her way onto the tiny landing beyond her side door and silently maneuvered it closed behind her. It was her first step onto the crunchy grass that alerted the crazy bird out front that she had gotten away. As she ran for her truck, keys clutched in her hand, Willard wobbled around the front side of the house, feathers still straight up in the air like Einstein's hair, and beat feet after her. She barely made it into the driver's seat and slammed the door shut before he appeared at her side.

"Ha! So there!"

God, she was as crazy as the bird. She'd lived alone far too long, apparently, if she was having conversations with Willard—and crowing her victory over him through the truck door.

Still, she couldn't keep herself from a little bounce in her seat as she backed out of the driveway and headed into town. Normally she'd be at JD's job site atop Black Wolf's Bluff today, but the crew from Nashville that was putting the steel frame in place had run into a delay due to their unusually wet autumn season, and nothing else could be done in the meantime, so for today at least, Erin was free. It didn't happen often, but she'd take it when she could.

Her watch hit half past by the time she pulled her truck into the restaurant parking lot. She hurried inside, feeling like a mess with her hair all over the place and sweat under her usual coveralls. Which was what she got for rushing off to town without removing her coat. The heater in the truck worked great—usually too great. A coat wasn't a necessity after the first three minutes of driving, but no, she'd been in a hurry.

And why did she care how she looked?

Fanning her heated cheeks, she jogged up to the usual table for her and Lily's weekly lunches and plopped down in the bench seat opposite one of her best friends. "I'm so sorry, Lily. I got caught up—"

Lily took in her ragged state over a queso-covered chip. "You need something besides that job to occupy your time," she mumbled around a bite.

"I wasn't—"

"I mean"—Lily swallowed the chip, simultaneously reaching for her margarita—"I get loving your job. Lord knows there's no other reason I'd put up with the crap that I do. But you let those guys take up way too much of your life."

Erin groaned. As if she hadn't heard this argument for years. "I am perfectly happy the way that I am."

"You are perfect the way that you are," Lily agreed. After a sip of her (what looked like) strawberry margarita, she dabbed at her lips before continuing. "That doesn't mean things couldn't be better. Work isn't all there is to life."

Erin sighed. "Work isn't all of my life. After all, I have you —*to annoy me*—"

11

Lily snickered.

"And Scarlett and Claire, not to mention Claire's goodies." She counted off on her fingers. "Then there's my in-laws, Maria and JD and now Linc, I guess, and Iris and Lou and—"

"Are you going to name everyone in town?"

Erin rolled her eyes. "Why not?"

"How about Clayton?"

Erin choked on the sip of water she'd taken from her water glass.

"You know," Lily went on, "Clay—"

"I know, I know." If her friends weren't reminding her, someone else in town was. "He's the most eligible bachelor around."

And despite being desperately handsome, the man drew absolutely no spark from her whatsoever.

"But that doesn't matter," she went on to say, pausing when Adrian stopped at their table. Besides being their usual waiter when they lunched at Casa Blanca, Adrian was also their friend Maria's son, and never failed to give them a hard time—as he proceeded to prove.

"So you finally showed up?"

Erin gave the young man her best matronly stare. "And?"

Adrian smirked. "And I can get you a margarita?"

"That better not be a question," Lily told him.

"Make it a strawberry," Erin added.

Adrian winked. "You got it. The usual for lunch?"

Erin nodded, waiting until Adrian had headed for the kitchen before turning back to Lily. Who picked up right where they'd left off.

"Why doesn't it matter?" Lily asked.

It took a moment before Erin could get back to her train of thought. "Ah! Because"—she paused dramatically just to irritate her friend—"apparently I've already been claimed."

Lily spit out her sip of margarita. Erin barely dodged the spray. "Hey, watch it!"

"You're what?" Lily choked.

Erin giggled. "I've already been claimed—by Willard."

"That crazy peacock?"

"The very one. He's actually why I'm late. I wasn't at the job site…" She raised a brow at Lily, who flushed guiltily. "I was at the house, and the damn bird wouldn't let me out. He's decided I'm his mate or something. As if he doesn't already have a harem hanging on his every move. If I don't manage to sneak out, he can have me holed up in the house for hours."

"But he's just a bird."

"Have you ever seen a peacock get aggressive?" Erin shuddered. "They're massive, and those talons are not just for decoration."

Lily nodded mock-thoughtfully. "Still, you can do better than a peacock." Then more seriously, ignoring Erin's howl of laughter, "With me and Claire both very much involved with our other halves, now we need to find one for you."

She knew Lily was teasing, but the thought sent a shaft of something she couldn't really identify—and didn't want to identify—through her heart. "God, not you too. Seems like everybody and their brother in town wants to throw some man at me."

"Sounds dangerous." Lily giggled, but then her gaze sharpened on something over Erin's shoulder and she grimaced. "Speaking of…"

"Erin!"

Erin's heart dropped.

"How's the food?" Big Rich asked as he came even with their table. The massive former high school quarterback—way back, if his pot belly and the gray in his mustache was any indication—had taken over the restaurant from his grandfather straight out of high school, and though Erin couldn't fault his food, he knew her in-laws very well, and that meant he had no problems poking into her social life. In fact the only time he came out from the kitchen was when he had someone else to introduce her to. After so many years, she would think he'd learn.

"You know it's good, Rich," Erin assured him. The big man smiled down at her like an indulgent grandfather—and since he'd been her husband's godfather, that wasn't far off.

From behind his back he pulled her margarita, which she grasped with eager hands. "Plain strawberry today, huh? You girls keep me on my toes finding new flavors to indulge you."

"I think Abril is the one doing that," Lily pointed out, waving to the older woman with the long black braid manning the bar across the room. Abril waved back.

"Well, she comes up with the ideas," Rich admitted reluctantly, practically blushing. "But I source the ingredients."

"Speaking of which," Erin put in, "when are we getting some more of that yummy prickly pear?"

"Just got a new order in!"

Too bad Tennessee didn't allow carry-out for cocktails, or she'd ask Abril for a to-go cup for later.

"So, Erin…" Big Rich rocked back on his heels.

Uh-oh, here it comes.

"My nephew just came in from California."

"Oh?" A sense of dread crept from her belly to her throat.

"Yeah, nice young man." Rich was about the only person who would equate Erin with *young*. Even her in-laws had gotten past that stage. "He doesn't really know anybody around here. Maybe I could set you up with him this weekend, get you to show him around town?"

Lily shot Erin a sympathetic look just beneath Rich's radar. Let's face it, if you were an *old maid*, like Erin and her friends had long been considered—all being single, or at least formerly single—people were always trying to hook them up with someone, thinking they needed something more than what they already had in their lives. Or her life, since Lily and Claire were now firmly attached. That old-fashioned perception that being single and in her forties made her an old maid never seemed to go away. At least she didn't have any cats or they'd be calling her the crazy cat lady.

Well, there was a barn cat that visited on occasion, but that old tom really belonged to her in-laws.

She mustered up her most appreciative smile. "I appreciate that, Rich, but I'm really busy with the project at the resort…"

"All work and no play," he pointed out.

They really did see her as a boring old maid, didn't they?

Erin tried to laugh it off. "That's very true. Unfortunately my play will have to wait until we get farther along in this project. But I appreciate the thought."

"Besides—" Lily gave Rich her best, brightest politician's smile. Erin narrowed her eyes, suspicion sparking. "Erin's new boyfriend won't want to share her."

An awkward pause followed Lily's words. Erin could see the battle in Rich's eyes—he wanted desperately to know who said boyfriend was, either because he was just nosy or to have the privilege of sharing the latest juicy bit of town gossip. He also wanted Erin to hook up with his nephew. The two needs duked it out as she watched, but the need for gossip won out. "Boyfriend?"

"Oh yes," Lily said before Erin could correct Rich's mistaken impression. "He's such a playboy, but he's fallen hard for our Erin." She reached across the table and patted Erin's hand indulgently. "We just love him for her."

Erin shot Lily a don't-take-this-too-far glance.

Big Rich didn't look like he was about to give up. "Well…" He drew the word out with obvious reluctance. "What was his name, you say?"

"Willard."

Erin was fighting hard not to giggle.

The stubble along Rich's jaw made a raspy sound as he

scrubbed a hand on it. "Maybe you can point him out to me. Y'all will be at the pub on Thursday, right?"

It was their weekly ritual, but Erin was now thinking about skipping it. "Uh…"

Lily jumped into the gap. "We will, although we're not sure if Willard can make it. He's so busy."

"Sounds like you two are a pair," Rich said, disapproval pulling the edges of his mouth down. What was it with people criticizing her work ethic lately? "Maybe we'll see you there." Another awkward pause settled over them while the big man stood there beside the table, seeming to be searching for something else to say, but then he nodded. "Okay. Enjoy the drinks!"

They assured him they would, and he headed back toward the kitchen.

Lily shook her head. "First Clay and then Willard and now Big Rich's nephew. How many men are you going to turn down this week?"

"As many as it takes for everyone to leave me alone."

Lily eyed her. "Yeah, you might be a lost cause." She winked. "After all, if you won't date Clayton, I don't think there's anybody else that could possibly spark your interest."

Erin groaned as Adrian arrived with their plates. "Eat. Then you can smother me in wedding talk." And hopefully forget about throwing Clayton her way.

"Oh, you're asking for it now!" Lily launched into a discussion about her latest decisions on the catering for her Christmas Day wedding, and Erin sat back with a sigh of relief. Finally, someone else's love life to discuss. Hers was fine, thank you very much. When was everyone going to accept that?

Of course, that didn't stop her from a little daydreaming when Lily moved on to tales of her wedding dress and the matching ribbons on her and JD's cake.

CHAPTER
Three

"Dad," Thad called from the back where he was strapped into the seat opposite Carter, "can we stop for an apple pie?"

Carter glanced at the golden arches outside his window as they swept past. "Nope. You had a shake with your chicken nuggets two hours ago, right after we left the airport. That's plenty of dessert."

"Are you sure?" That wheedle only ten-year-olds could perfect sneaked into his son's voice. "I don't remember a shake. I think I had apple juice."

Thad said the words *apple juice* like he'd say *rancid milk*. He hated apple juice.

So did his dad.

Carter chuckled. "No apple juice. We swapped it out, remember?"

Oh, Thad remembered, but he'd get around it if he could. Carter didn't normally give him a lot of sugar, but a milk-shake had seemed like the perfect way for a ten-year-old to begin his vacation. A shake and an apple pie, though? He'd be bouncing off the ceiling of the SUV before they got twenty feet down the road.

The sound of Thad's sneakers banging into the bottom of his seat was a sure sign of boredom. Carter didn't enjoy being strapped in most of the day either, but a quick glance at his phone said they were almost at JD's house.

"The GPS says ten minutes, son. Just a little while longer, I promise."

Grumbling came from the back seat, but Carter gave it a pass and focused on the road. It had been raining since just outside of Nashville, and navigating the wet curves made him nervous with Thad in the car. He'd been sure to rent an SUV for the extra room and the four-wheel drive, but the strangeness of drenched, winding roads so unlike the ones at home and an unfamiliar rental car had intensified his awareness of the need to be careful.

A glance into the rearview mirror told him Thad was looking out the window too, into the woods, which was all there was to see. Carter could read the fascination in his son's eyes as he stared out at a landscape that was certainly nothing like their New York apartment and its surroundings.

"Is Uncle JD's place all trees and stuff?"

"He has a lot of land just like this, he told me. Once it dries up outside, we can do some exploring." After Carter talked to JD about snakes and mountain lions and bears or whatever other hazards might await unsuspecting city slickers in the woods. "Hey, JD says they built a firepit in the courtyard behind the house. Maybe we can roast some marshmallows one night."

More kicking of the seat. "Do they have sugar-free marshmallows?"

Carter felt a melting sensation in the center of his chest. Whenever Thad had a treat, he was adamant that his dad be able to join in. But Carter was a type one diabetic, so sugary carbs were 95 percent a no-no. At McD's that had meant a Diet Coke instead of a shake, and s'mores would mean sugar-free marshmallows and chocolate. Carter and Rachel had kept a close watch on Thad for issues with his blood sugar, but luckily so far he had tested totally normal, for which Carter was so damn grateful. "I'm sure someplace has them." If they didn't, Amazon delivered.

The turnoff up the mountain appeared, and Carter slowed to make a left. JD had warned him that the road was under construction, in the process of widening so that traffic could get to and from the resort, but the crew hadn't gotten far yet. Right now the drive was narrow, with no room for passing. A wide plane of construction on one side showed where the new lanes would be, but for now that area was a swath of running water rushing down the mountain, as was the drop-off on the opposite side. The setup reminded him of the one-car lanes he'd encountered all over Scotland when he visited his business partner, Gavin, there. Thad hadn't been with him then, though, and he took extra care to keep the SUV centered as they made their way to the top of what JD had told him was the mountain that lent the town of Black Wolf's Bluff its name.

As the road leveled out, he took a deep breath, blowing out his tension, and rounded what he hoped was the last curve before they reached the mansion. Out of nowhere, a massive red truck barreled around the blind corner, skidding to a stop dangerously close to the SUV. Carter slammed on the brakes, curses ringing through the air as he gave Thad a frantic glance in the rearview mirror. The white fear on Thad's face had anger flashing through Carter's chest.

Throwing the SUV into park, he reached between the seats with a shaking hand and gripped Thad's knee, the bone so small and fragile beneath his fingers. "We're all right, buddy. Everything's okay." He needed the reassurance almost as much as his son did, but since the divorce last year, surprises tended to set Thad off, as if he wondered what part of his life could fall apart next. He'd been slowly regaining his equilibrium, and had done remarkably well for this trip, but now... Carter squeezed down. "It's okay. Are you hurt?"

Thad shook his head, lip trembling. One small hand latched on to Carter's.

"It's fine now. Just a little surprise around the corner. Didn't expect that." He tried to laugh it off, though the sound was tight from the anger squeezing his chest. Whatever dumbass had been driving that truck—

Thad still clutched his hand, but the color was returning to his cheeks. "It's okay." Thad drew himself up as if proving the words to himself as well as Carter, and Carter's gut knotted to match his chest. Thad nodded. "I'm okay, Dad." Cautious eyes looked beyond Carter out of the windshield.

So did Carter. His gaze narrowed on the blurred face behind the steering wheel of the truck. "Let me—"

Just as he was about to release Thad and step out of the SUV, intent on giving the other driver a piece of his mind, the truck began to reverse up the drive. Carter grunted, irritation flaring that the object of his anger was backing away without the chance to ream them for putting his son in danger. Nonetheless, he put the SUV in drive and followed the truck about a quarter mile until the road flattened out just before a set of massive iron gates. The truck backed farther, allowing space for Carter to turn between the gates, entering the circular drive before JD's mansion. As he did so, a quick glance showed him what looked like a young girl in a flannel shirt, brunette braids falling over each shoulder. Jesus, was she even old enough to drive?

He pulled to a stop, but before he could jump out, the truck had surged forward just behind him and hurried back down the mountain. Carter grumbled under his breath, too low for Thad to pick out any curse words, as he circled around to park just outside the front door.

The quiet that followed the engine dying quickly filled with the patter of rain on the roof. Carter forced a deep breath, forced his focus off what had just happened and back on Thad. "We're here, buddy."

A glance toward the house showed the enormous oak door opening and one of his best friends in the world, JD Lane, and a slender woman he assumed was Lily, JD's fiancée, moving onto the wide front steps to greet them. Now that he was paying more attention, he noticed the gray stone building was more castle in architecture than country home, with a turret-style entrance embedded in the center of long wings stretching out on either side. A small overhang protected JD and Lily from the falling rain, but as Carter watched, JD left his fiancée behind to hurry toward them, a huge black umbrella opening in his hands.

His friend jogged around to the driver's side and stood waiting as Carter exited into the safety of the umbrella's cover. The two men clasped opposite hands, their shoulders coming together in a classic bro hug.

"Glad you're finally here," JD said, grinning.

"Barely," Carter huffed. "Someone nearly took us out at the last minute."

"What?"

Carter slammed his door shut behind him. "Some asshole in a huge truck almost hit us outside the gates."

JD's frown turned into a shake of his head. "Must've been Erin; she was the only one here today." He glanced over his shoulder. "That's not like her. Normally she's the most careful person I know, but Lily said she just got a call about a family emergency."

"That shouldn't entail putting others in danger." Carter gave Thad a significant look through the window where he'd climbed from his seat to the driver's side.

"No, it shouldn't," JD agreed, reaching to open the door for Thad to clamber out. "You're totally right. I'm sure she'll apologize when she gets back. She wasn't aware you were arriving this afternoon."

"She's coming back?"

"Of course. She's our contractor."

What the hell kind of hick town was this where women that young called themselves general contractors?

Oblivious to Carter's shock, JD was hustling them around the front bumper of the SUV, umbrella covering all three of them. "Leave the suitcases; we'll come back for them."

Carter stayed silent as they mounted the steps, one hand on Thad's shoulder in case he slipped on the slick stone. Lily was waiting with open arms.

"Carter!" She quickly pulled him to her, the force of her personality far stronger than her slender arms. "It's so good to finally meet you in person. JD talks about you all the time."

"What about me?" Thad piped up as Carter and Lily parted.

Lily knelt before Thad, her hand coming up to shake. "I've heard about you too, Thad. I'm Lily."

Thad shook the woman's hand solemnly, putting on his best adult face. The sight allowed amusement to filter through Carter's still-simmering anger.

"Nice to meet you, Aunt Lily," his son said.

Lily's eyes softened at the nickname. "I'm honored, Thad. Thank you."

Thad's ten-year-old enthusiasm broke through the solemnity, and he nearly bowled Lily off her feet throwing his arms around her neck to give her a big hug.

JD finished shaking out the umbrella and ushered them through the open door. "Let's get in out of the rain."

In the marble-floored foyer, they doffed their wet shoes and padded down the hall in their socked feet to a massive kitchen Carter knew had been recently remodeled.

JD took orders for hot chocolate from Thad and black coffee for Carter to warm them both up. As Lily filled the coffeepot for the adults, JD explained to his fiancée about their run-in with the so-called contractor earlier.

"You've got to be kidding me, JD," Carter finally burst out. "No way is that girl old enough to be our contractor."

But Lily laughed at Carter's words. "Remember that when she comes back." She turned on the pot to brew and moved to join them on the stools to one side of the massive center island. Carter was beginning to think *massive* described everything about the mansion. "Every woman wants to be told how young she looks."

Carter arched a brow. "Just looks?"

"Your radar is definitely off, bro." JD crossed to place a steaming mug of cocoa before Thad. "Dating too many young women, Carter? Blow on that before you drink it, Thad." He jerked his chin toward Lily. "Erin and Lily are the same age."

Remembering the braids framing either side of the woman's face, Carter was tempted to call his friend a damn liar, but he held his tongue. Maybe he'd seen wrong in that quick glance into the truck. At any rate, he had other things to take up with this Erin that had nothing to do with her age— like reckless driving.

In the meantime, he had a son to settle in. Their vacation may have gotten off to a rough start, but he intended to make the most of this time with Thad.

"Try this," JD ordered, offering him a full mug of deep black coffee.

Carter took a sip, and his tastebuds started singing. "What is it?"

"Gift from Linc," JD told him as he settled on the stool next to Lily's. "Guatemalan special blend."

"Of course." Leave it to Linc to find a hidden treasure like this nectar from the gods. He felt the stress in his shoulders and neck begin to ease as he sipped from his cup, Thad's chatter flowing over him as he set about getting to know his new aunt. Carter needed to get the bags from the SUV and get their vacation started, and he would. Right after he warmed up with the best damn coffee he'd had in a long, long time.

CHAPTER

Four

Erin's heart raised ninety to nothing as she rushed through the slowly opening door of the ER at the small county hospital in the next town over from Black Wolf's Bluff. Her hometown was too small to have their own hospital, but Erin had spent enough time at this one to be familiar with where everything was. She was at the registration desk before she could catch her next hurried breath.

"Scott Jenkins, please. He came in about an hour ago." The words were ragged, but she managed to force them out.

The nurse barely glanced up. "Family only."

Erin gritted her teeth. "I am family."

This time the woman took a longer look, then sighed. "Mr. Jenkins has his wife with him. He doesn't need anyone else."

Erin's control snapped. "He needs his daughter. Now either take me there or go get Ruth and she'll tell you who I am."

The woman glared, and Erin thought for one nearly hysterical second that she would refuse, but after a moment of hesitation she got out of her seat and went to the back, hopefully to get Ruth and not a security guard. Erin was preparing herself for a fight when her mother-in-law pushed through the double doors leading back to the ER cubicles.

Thank God. Erin felt her entire body sag with relief but pushed herself to hurry, rushing to Ruth's side. Her mother-in-law gathered her to her chest immediately, no doubt absorbing the shaking Erin had been unable to stop since she'd read Ruth's message. "Where is he?"

Ruth cupped the back of her head lovingly and pulled her closer, something she used to do when Erin was younger and grieving over her parents. That touch more than anything told her Ruth understood the memories running through Erin's head, the fears, the horror that she would lose anyone else in her life.

"He's right back here, dear. It's all right."

It wasn't, but Erin didn't argue as Ruth led her down the hallway. The nurse from the registration desk passed them on her way out, her nasty look saying she didn't like that she'd been overridden by Ruth and Scott, but who the hell cared. Erin needed to see her father-in-law, not follow some stupid policy that kept people separated when they needed all the love they could get.

"There's my girl," Scott said as they pushed the curtain aside to enter his cubicle. "I knew you'd be here anytime."

Erin tucked her sudden nausea back down into her stomach, taking in the sight of Scott in the hospital bed, oxygen tube under his nose, blood pressure cuff squeezing down on his bicep, an IV in his opposite arm. Beeps and whooshing filled the space, stirring the monsters at the back of her mind, but she shut those off too and hurried to the side of the bed. "Why didn't you call me when you weren't feeling well, Dad?"

She probably shouldn't be reprimanding him, but for God's sake, they'd waited till he got to the hospital to tell her anything was wrong. She could've lost him without ever seeing him again.

Scott opened his arms wide, and Erin wanted to throw herself into them, comfort herself with the hug that had comforted her for twenty-three years, but instead she eased herself in, not wanting to disrupt the lines and wires attached to his seventy-year-old body. The reassurance of his hug enveloped her, and the steady beat of his heart beneath her cheek eased some of her panic. "I'm going to be fine, Bug," Scott murmured, the words gravelly with what she knew was pain.

The use of his nickname for her, the one that had naturally appeared after she began dating their son, Stephen, in her freshman year of high school, squeezed her heart. Ruth and Scott had been her family now for more years than her parents had been able to share with her. They'd died her senior year of high school, and Scott and Ruth had not just taken her in but welcomed her with open arms into their home and their lives. Erin and Stephen had married the very next year, and Scott and Ruth had become her family, not just her in-laws. Even when Stephen died of a heart attack, leaving her a widow, he hadn't left her alone; his family was hers.

She eased back from Scott, clearing the roughness from her throat. "What happened?"

"He was tossing hay from the loft of the barn," Ruth said, her tone harsh.

Scott closed his eyes as if he'd heard that accusation more than once today. "The horses needed to be fed."

"Where was Gary?" Erin demanded. She'd hired the man herself to take over the tasks on the farm that Scott shouldn't do anymore but wouldn't give up without someone to take his place.

"Didn't show up," Scott growled. One hand came up to rub at his chest, making Erin's stomach roll all over again.

"Again?"

Ruth sat in the chair next to hers and patted her hand

gently. "It's not your fault, Erin."

Her mother-in-law knew her so well, but she was wrong. This was her fault. She'd hired Gary, figuring the twentysomething handyman could use the work as much as Scott needed the help, and now she'd have to hire someone else after she fired the damn man. The weight of responsibility made her shoulders sag for a moment before she determinedly squared them.

"What does the doctor say?"

"The doctor says Mr. Jenkins has pulled a chest muscle."

The deep voice came from the vicinity of the curtain closing Scott's cubicle off from the others in the ER. Erin looked up to meet a pair of glittering gray eyes in a chiseled face. She'd grown up in the area, knew nearly everyone who lived in a thirty-mile radius of Black Wolf's Bluff—it wasn't like they got new blood that often, although with the resort opening, that would likely change. The eyes staring back at her weren't familiar, however.

"Where's Dr. Barnard?" she asked involuntarily.

"Dr. Barnard is retiring," the new doctor said, stepping fully into the cubicle. He was tall, muscled beneath his khakis and lab coat, his dark hair sprinkled with white strands. The smile he gave her as he held out his hand was kind. "I'm the cardiologist who'll be taking over his practice, Dr. Marshall."

Given Stephen's issues with his heart, along with both Scott's and Ruth's advancing ages, their family had been under Dr. Barnard's care for a couple of decades. The man was as old as her in-laws, but somehow the idea of him retiring had never entered her mind. "You're new to the area."

It wasn't a question, and Dr. Marshall nodded as if he was used to it. In as rural an area as theirs, he probably was. His tilted lips said he took no offense. "My wife and I moved a couple of weeks ago."

That explained it. But back to the matter at hand. "You

said Scott has pulled a muscle?"

"Yes." Walking to the bedside, he addressed his patient. "Aside from a bit of stress, which is what's got your heart rate and blood pressure elevated, your heart is fine, Mr. Jenkins. It appears as if the pectoralis minor muscle on your left side has a tear in it, likely from lifting more than you should. With time and rest, it will heal just fine."

Scott grimaced at the words *time and rest*, Erin noticed. She glared down at him. "And no more lifting."

His gaze glanced off hers. "Someone has to do it."

She knew he didn't mean it the way she took it, but she winced anyway. "I'll take care of the horses and Bessie until I can hire someone else."

"But Gary…"

Ruth's voice faded as she caught the flash of anger in Erin's eyes. "Gary should've shown up when he was supposed to. Scott could have been seriously hurt."

The thought almost brought her to her knees. If something serious had happened to him, if he'd suffered a heart attack like Stephen…

The memory flashed in her mind without warning— Stephen lying in a hospital bed just like this one. The nasal cannula that had provided him with oxygen was slightly askew, the BP cuff tight across his arm as it assessed a heart-beat that was no longer there. The sheet covering his pale skin was mussed, the gown pulled open to reveal a muscled chest that should have protected a healthy heart. But Stephen's heart hadn't been healthy, and in that moment in her memory, neither had it been beating. Her handsome husband had died in a hospital bed just like Scott's, and it was a moment that would haunt her for the rest of her life.

She shoved the memory deep down, along with her pain over her husband's too-young death, and focused on Scott. "I'll take care of it, Dad. I promise."

"And I'd like you to see me to follow up," Dr. Marshall

28

inserted.

"Thought you said I was fine," Scott grumped.

"I said you are fine for now." He made a note on the electronic tablet in his hand. "I didn't say you would stay fine if we don't get that BP and heart rate under control."

His patient scowled. "I don't like to take medicine."

Dr. Marshall pointed Ruth and Erin's way. "Do you love them?"

Scott glanced at them, and Erin could read the memories in his eyes as sure as she could feel them hovering just below the surface of her mind. Scott and Ruth knew very well how serious heart problems could get. Stephen had suffered from a congenital heart defect no one had detected until he went out for high school football, but you didn't have to have something wrong from birth for a problem with your heart to kill you.

The lines in Scott's face relaxed as he searched her eyes, then latched on to Ruth's. "I do."

"Good." Dr. Marshall nodded sharply. He took a pad of paper out of the breast pocket of his coat and began to scribble something on it. "Then you'll take the medicine." Tearing off the sheet, he handed the paper to Scott. "Call my office tomorrow."

"Thank you, Doctor," Ruth said kindly.

"You bet." With a quick, warm smile, Dr. Marshall exited the cubicle, leaving Erin grateful. Dr. Barnard had tried for a couple of years to get Scott on BP meds, but the man was as stubborn as an ox. Maybe the scare of the ER visit had combined with just the right words to finally get through to him.

A nurse bustled in to get Scott ready to leave, and Erin excused herself to run outside and call Lily. No way would she be returning to the work site today. She had a dad to get home and get settled, and a hired hand to fire—and two old horses and a grumpy cow named Bessie to feed come dark.

CHAPTER

Five

"Come on, Dad!"

"He has way too much energy in the mornings," JD said beside him as they trudged up the
muddy path toward the build site.

Carter couldn't say anything. He'd already traversed the
paved portion of the drive down the mountain twice this
morning to get his run in now that the rain had finally
stopped. Yesterday they'd stayed inside, listening to the rain
and playing board games until Thad had retreated to his
tablet to read. At that point Carter had picked up the thriller
he'd brought along and they'd spent several hours reading
and napping in the warmth of the living room until it had
been time to help with dinner.

Those quiet moments with his son soothed his heart.
Those were the moments he missed more than anything when
Thad was spending his required weeks with his mother. He
didn't think he'd ever get used to only being physically with
his son part-time, although he strove to be an everyday part
of his son's life no matter where Thad was.

But this morning had broken with a brilliant sunrise. After
his run, he'd spent a messy hour teaching Thad to make

pancakes—why was flipping those floppy, flat disks so hard? —and then they'd donned some galoshes JD had the foresight to buy and come outside to explore. Because of the rain, it would be a couple of days before any outside construction could continue, which made it the perfect time to tour the resort site.

Thad was a bit more anxious to get there than the adults.

"I think you've gotten too used to being away from the office," Carter said.

JD hmphed. "Hey, why not take advantage of flexible hours while you have them."

And a beautiful fiancée to spend them with. Not that Carter envied JD and Lily, but he remembered that stage of a relationship. Late nights and early mornings spent in bed but not asleep. He was happy for his friend, but he was currently content with having Thad wake him up early on Monday mornings instead of a woman.

He grimaced at the sucking sound his galoshes made as he pulled them from the mud. The expanded road would extend all the way up here to the lodge, but not until the ground firmed enough for work to continue. Thad was taking turns tromping along and using running starts to send him skiing along the surface of the mess. The sheer joy on his son's face was worth the cleanup they'd face when they got back to the mansion.

"The permits took a while to secure," JD was saying, "but we broke ground in August. There will eventually be multiple sites on the acreage, including a ski area—"

"Skiing?" Thad yelled more than asked.

JD gave him an indulgent smile. "Skiing. We're already working on hiking paths through the woods, and possibly a stable and horseback riding eventually." He turned back to Carter. "For now, though, we're focused on the main lodge."

Carter remembered that from the discussions he'd sat in on. The 130-room hotel would be in *upscale rustic style,* whatever that meant, but JD seemed enthusiastic about it. Although Carter was an investor, he didn't have his friend's same excitement when it came to building. He'd save his excitement for when he could bring Thad back to stay at the completed lodge. Thad was the one currently bubbling over with delight as they came into view of a huge crane and several other pieces of heavy machinery. Steel beams and stacks of materials the crew were slowly putting together to frame the enormous building dotted the site, along with a massive expanse of gray concrete. Oh, and a whole lot of mud.

JD slid a bit, then righted himself with a grunt. "They'll need a couple more days for things to dry out before they get back to work, obviously."

"Will they be working while we're here?" Thad asked as they stepped onto the flat gray surface of the foundation. Both hands fiddled with the too large hard hat he wore. Carter had already taken pictures—that tiny face peeking out from beneath the yellow plastic had been too adorable to resist. He'd text the pictures to Rachel later, after they were inside again and he didn't have to add her maternal worries on top of his own anxiety about bringing a ten-year-old to a construction site, active or not.

JD had no such anxiety, probably because he didn't have kids. And Carter had to admit that the huge steel beams, some already welded into place—or whatever it was they did with steel beams—and some still stacked a good couple of stories high around the building site, were pretty impressive. He adjusted his own hard hat at an angle that allowed him to see the beams that would support the roof several stories above them.

"We want the lodge to feel as much a part of the woods as possible," JD explained. "It'll end up being smaller than we wanted, but we plan to add a second, smaller location later to supplement."

Carter eyed the surrounding trees. "I admit I wasn't too sure about the decision from all the way up in New York, but seeing it now, actually standing in the environment, I totally understand."

"It's definitely a different feel from a high-rise in New York City."

"Our apartment is way up high," Thad put in. "Way higher than this."

"Yeah," JD said, "but look at what else we have: trees, mountains… We even have deer and bears."

The word *bears* sent a shiver down Carter's spine. "And that's why you have to stay near the mansion," he reminded Thad. "No running off into the woods without one of us, okay?"

"Are bears dangerous? They look so cute on TV."

JD's words were serious, imparting the importance of what he was about to say. "They are dangerous. I didn't know it at first either, but even the little cubs that look like teddy bears are dangerous. And where cubs are, mama bears are sure to follow, and they're the most dangerous of all."

"Oh." Thad seemed to consider that. "Okay. But can I see a deer?"

JD chuckled. "I'll take you over to meet Lily's granddad. He knows all about wildlife. He can show you some pretty neat things."

"Yay!"

Carter laughed at his son's enthusiasm.

They skirted well around the areas that had been dug out for basement locations—laundries, storage, and that type of thing, Carter assumed. Temporary barriers had been placed for safety, but Carter gave Thad another warning, just in case. No coming up to the build site without an adult. His son nodded, his eyes huge as he stared down into the pits from a safe distance away.

At the opposite end of the giant build, Carter took a

moment to turn and stare back toward the mansion and beyond, to the valley below the mountain. Maybe a hundred yards downhill from the edge of the foundation, he noticed what looked like an old shed sitting near the end of a turnoff he'd barely noticed on their way up. Its outer walls were covered in timeworn lumber, the roof made of corrugated tin that was more rust than metal at this point. It looked like a stiff wind would blow it right down. He nodded toward the building. "Is that original to the land?"

"It is." JD chuckled. "The crew wanted to tear it down before they got started, but Erin insisted on keeping it for the time being. She uses it as her shop for now. It'll disappear when the landscaping starts to come in."

Erin. The woman JD had said was driving the truck on Saturday. Wisps of the anger he'd held against her ever since then began to trace across his mind.

Just as he was about to say something, the rumble of a heavy engine reached them. A truck. Carter's eyes narrowed.

"Well, speak of the devil." JD grinned, then glanced down at Thad. "How about we go meet the woman responsible for all this?"

Thad followed willingly, oblivious to Carter's hesitation. "You mean a girl is in charge of all this stuff?" His little hand waved behind them toward the building site.

"Absolutely!"

"Even the big crane?"

JD cocked a brow down at Thad. "Don't you think girls can build stuff as well as boys can?"

Thad considered that very seriously. "I guess so. Samantha in my class is always drawing pictures of buildings and apartments and things. I just never thought about her building them."

"Wait till you see Erin on one of those big bulldozers," JD told him. "She's better than any of those boys at running that thing."

"Cool! Think she'd let me go for a ride?"

"No way, son."

Thad threw a pout over his shoulder. "Ah, Dad, why not?"

"Because your mom would skin me alive if she found out I let you do something that dangerous." And no way in hell would he willingly watch Thad ride one of those monster bulldozers either.

JD threw over his shoulder, "Party pooper."

Thad opened his mouth, probably to agree with JD, but the sound of the truck door slamming shut distracted him. He turned back around, then began a jog through the brush toward the woman making her way into the shed not too far from them now.

Carter took the extra time to examine the woman in front of him. Tall, though not as tall as him. The blue-jean coveralls and thick flannel shirt she wore obscured a lot, but her figure was lean, athletic. Once again he found himself doubting JD's knowledge of the woman's age. Her face had a timeless quality, making her seem younger despite the fact that the braids from Saturday had been traded in for a ponytail at the back of her head that struggled to hold the abundance of warm brown strands that complemented her tanned complexion nicely. Not that he wanted to notice her complexion or how nice it was. He reminded himself that this was the woman who'd almost run them off the road mere days ago; a nice face and body wasn't going to make up for that kind of miscalculation in judgment.

Neither JD nor Thad seemed to have similar misgivings. In fact his son ran right up to the woman, presenting his hand with an enthusiasm that sparked a surprising bite of jealousy in Carter's chest. "Hi, I'm Thad."

The woman smiled down at Thad and took his hand with enthusiasm. "Hi, Thad. I'm Erin."

"You're the construction girl," Thad said.

Erin winked. "I'm the construction boss."

JD laughed as he joined the pair. "Indeed you are."

Erin glanced up at her employer. Eyes the color of forest moss snagged JD's, then flitted to Carter's face. Those eyes widened when they met his.

He felt the impact deep in his bones, a jolt of electricity that took his breath away and replaced it with an acute discomfort in his groin that threw gasoline on the smoldering anger he still held. He wasn't attracted to this woman. He wasn't. He was here to spend time with his son, not have his hormones go crazy over some reckless woman he shouldn't be noticing at all.

"Hello," Erin said, her voice softer than it had been with Thad.

He frowned. "Hello."

A vee appeared between Erin's brows. The moment drew out until JD cleared his throat. "Erin, this is my friend Carter."

She reached a hand out to shake. "I recognize you from JD's pictures."

Carter didn't respond verbally. He didn't want to respond physically either—Erin's hand might as well have been a snake—but he forced himself to be polite.

He should have listened to his instincts. The moment her hand, stronger and rougher than even most men he'd known, slid against his, he felt a fascination rise up inside of him. He wanted to know why her hands were rough. Why she had to be this strong. He wanted—

Shit.

"I think you recognized me from almost mowing us down two days ago."

JD growled low in his throat, obviously displeased with Carter's rudeness. Carter couldn't tell him it was all self-defense.

For the briefest moment Erin seemed at a loss for words.

Then her shoulders squared and her mouth firmed. "Yes, I apologize. That was certainly irresponsible of me."

"And understandable," JD cut in. "You thought your dad had had a heart attack."

And now Carter felt like even more of a dick. But maybe that was better than playing Mr. Nice Guy. After all, he'd played Mr. Nice Guy with his sister, and look where that had gotten him. Being propositioned for a role as *daddy*. He should have learned his lesson by now.

"Nonetheless," Erin said, her voice stiff, "it won't happen again."

"Good."

Yea, definitely a dick. JD glared at him for a moment before turning back to Erin. "We were touring the site. Want to join us?"

Her gaze bounced off Carter's chest before returning to JD. "Sorry, I have some things I need to take care of." A vague wave toward the shack said those things were work.

Thad frowned. "Won't you come with us? Uncle JD said you knew everything about the big crane and bulldozer."

Erin smiled down at him. "We can take a look at those another time, okay, Thad? I'd be happy to let you sit in the cabin—while the machinery is off, of course. Safety first!"

Her chipper tone eased Thad's displeasure. As Erin entered the shed and the three of them headed back up the mountain, Carter mulled over the influence she seemed to have over his child. It looked like not only did he need to keep himself away from her, but Thad as well. The few days they had here were for the two of them, not the two of them and some woman.

He'd have to make sure of it.

CHAPTER
Six

E rin's day started at four thirty, long before the first streaks of autumn light appeared on the horizon. Bessie wasn't waiting any longer than that to be fed and milked, and the chorus of her loud mooing and the horses nickering and bumping at the gate of their pasture— conveniently right near her house, on the same side as her bedroom window—woke her far before her alarm. Dragging on clothes in the dark was accompanied with fumbling and curses, but finally she was ready to walk over and feed the animals. She then spent a good twenty minutes with her fore-head pressed against Bessie's warm belly while she filled the milk pail with the daily offering. The fact that Scott was securing the clasps of his overalls at his shoulders, ready to head out to the barn, when she brought in the milk only emphasized the need to replace Gary as soon as possible. Her father-in-law was definitely stubborn.

Maybe being around him so much was where she got it from.

From there it was on to the job site, a trip Erin made easily since Willard was busy scratching at the feed she'd laid out before heading toward her truck. The crew spent the morning adding to the steel frame of the lodge. Between supervising and spelling some of her guys on the equipment so they could have breaks, she spent her time on e-mails to vendors and phone calls with everyone on the planet, it seemed. But noon finally came, and she was determined to take her lunch break just like her crew.

A couple of years after they married, Stephen had helped her convert their small barn into a workshop. Woodworking had always been her hobby, and even now, working as a general contractor, she found it soothing to build things in her off time, albeit on a smaller scale than she did during her workdays. But she couldn't get back to her house every day for lunch, so she'd asked JD's permission to convert a small shed on the property—although the term *shed* might be a bit too glamorous for the old lean-to—into a workspace that she could putter around in during breaks.

Her current project, a new tiered display stand for Claire's latest addition to the bakery's menu, macarons, was coming along nicely. Erin was running the sander over the butcher block boards she intended to cut for the individual trays when she heard the telltale shriek of the old door being pulled open behind her.

Powering down the sander was the work of a moment, as was pulling up her safety glasses, but by the time she turned around, a figure half her size was right in front of her. "Oh, hello."

"Hi!"

She had to admit, Thadeus Deveraux was adorable. His wide grin was missing a couple of teeth on the side, and the mop of dark blond, curly hair on his head made her fingers itch to touch it to see if it was as soft as it looked. His blue eyes sparkled with life, although she could see depths there that she thought hid pain. Carter was divorced, Lily had said. Fairly recently, too. Had his parents' breakup put those shadows in Thad's beautiful eyes?

"Thad, right?" she asked, returning his grin. "How are you doing today?"

"Good!"

Everything he said seemed to come with an exclamation point. She could hear it in his voice, in the little jump his body gave when he responded. It was absolutely the cutest thing she'd ever seen.

A glance behind the boy showed nothing but clear space. "Where's your dad?" Carter was the exact opposite of his son. The man had a glower that would rain on anyone's parade. It certainly cut the "cute" factor where he was concerned. How he'd managed to produce a kid as beautiful—and happy—as Thad was beyond her.

"He went for his run. He goes every day."

Of course he did. Why that irked her, she had no idea.

Curious eyes took in her workshop. "Is it okay for me to be in here? I'm not bothering you, am I?"

"It's fine for you to be in here as long as I am, okay?" She raised her eyebrows at him until he gave her a solemn nod. The contrast with his normal exuberance told her he was taking her seriously. "And absolutely no going up to the work site unless you've got your dad or another adult with you. It can be really dangerous."

"Dad already told me." He looked at the wood sitting on the table in front of her. "Whatcha makin'?"

Erin ran a gloved hand over the still-rough lamination. "I'm making a display stand for a friend of mine. Have you ever seen anyone put a cake on a little pedestal with a glass bowl over it?"

Thad's brow wrinkled. "I don't think so."

"How about cupcakes?"

The wrinkles smoothed out. "Not at home—we don't have cake at home much. But at restaurants, yeah!"

Somehow the idea of not allowing a little boy cake fit right in with her impression of Carter. Ignoring the comment, she tilted the block of wood up for Thad to see. "Well, this is sort of like that. See the lines?" She traced her finger over the join between each individual length of wood. "I glued them all together into what is called butcher block. And now I'm sanding it to get rid of any splinters or things that would catch on people's fingers or food."

"Can I touch it?"

"Sure." She watched him run his fingers over the wood. "I'm going to sand this down till it's completely smooth, and then I'll be cutting circles out of it, and several more pieces like it, to stack on top of each other in tiers." She demonstrated with her hands. "Then my friend can put cupcakes or pastries or whatever she wants on them."

This particular butcher block was made from scraps of wood she'd had lying around her shop at home. The rich yellow of the poplar, creamy white of the maple, and reddish-brown of the birch contrasted beautifully to make a pattern she thought would be a lovely complement to the shop's interior. And the trees were all native to their local woods. "Have you been to the bakery in town?"

Thad shook his head. "Uh-uh."

Of course not. "My friend Claire owns it. It's called Gimme Sugar." The name made Thad laugh. "She has lots of great goodies there."

"Does she make sugar-free stuff?"

Carter had a real hard-on for not giving this kid sugar, didn't he? "I don't know, but I bet she does. She has all kinds of treats."

Thad nodded. His curious gaze going back to the wood, he asked, "Can I help you?"

"How about you watch me for a few minutes, and then I can supervise if you want to try it?"

There went the little bounce again. "Great!"

"First, you have to wear safety glasses." She pointed to the ones on her head. "Always wear safety glasses when you're doing anything in a workshop or on a construction site."

"I wore a hard hat the other day. Do I need to wear a hard hat in here?"

She chuckled as she searched on her makeshift desk—a piece of plywood laid over two sawhorses—for an extra pair of glasses. "No hard hat in here. Hard hats are for when heavy stuff could fall on your head."

"Oh. That makes sense."

She got Thad settled with the glasses, making extra sure that his eyes were protected and that he stood back far enough that he wasn't in danger of any flying splinters. "Now just watch for a minute and see what I'm doing." She tilted the sander to one side and pointed at the strip of paper secured to the bottom. "See this?"

Thad nodded vigorously.

"This is sandpaper, and when I turn the sander on"—she flipped the palm-sized machine until the sandpaper was facing the wood—"it vibrates the paper so that it sands faster than I can do it by hand." She flipped on the machine and applied it to the wood, moving in slow circles to polish any bumps or dents or splinters from the surface. Thad watched quietly, and each time she glanced at him, his gaze was intent on her work as if he could absorb how to do it by sheer willpower. The kid definitely seemed to enjoy learning new things.

After a couple of minutes she flipped the sander off. "Wanna try?"

"Yes!"

She didn't have a step stool in the shop, but she found a block of wood that would give Thad a little more height, allowing him a better angle to see what they were doing. After he stepped up, she moved in beside him. "Are you left-handed or right-handed?"

"Right-handed."

"Good. So am I." She smiled down at him as she took his hand. "Place your palm here"—she laid his hand on top of the sander—"and I'll help guide you after I turn the machine on. You have to hold it tight at first," she warned, "because sometimes it wants to run away from you."

Thad laughed. The sound did something funny to her heart.

"Ready?"

Thad glanced up at her, his smile lighting up his whole face. "Ready!"

And that was how JD and Carter found them, a long time later, running the sander over and over the butcher block until it was ultrasmooth. Unfortunately Carter didn't look as smooth as the wood they were working on. Hearing the door squeak, Erin glanced up automatically, her mind still mostly on Thad, to be greeted by the infamous Carter Deveraux glower, as she was coming to think of it.

She lifted the sander from the wood and powered it down. Thad bounced on his block of wood. "Look at it! It's so neat."

"Thad."

At least he wasn't barking at the boy. Still, Erin could feel her own frown deepen as she lifted her safety glasses. Removing the barrier only made the displeasure on Carter's face clearer.

Thad lifted his glasses as well. "Dad, look! We're making butcher block." He glanced up at Erin. "That's what you call it, right?"

She gave the boy a smile. "That's what you call it." With her gloved hand, she dusted the bits of debris from the surface to give a clear view of the beautiful slab beneath. "You've done a good job, Thad."

"We've been looking everywhere for you," Carter said sharply. Erin would've jumped down his throat for that if she hadn't caught a glimpse of fear in Carter's face. Thad had gone missing; she could understand how that would affect a

43

dad, even if she did feel her hackles rise anytime she was in the man's vicinity.

Thad's shoulders slumped. "I just came to see Erin. I didn't go to the building site, I promise."

"You didn't tell me you were leaving the courtyard," JD said, his voice gentler than his friend's. "I wasn't sure where you were."

"I'm sorry." Thad shook his head and glanced over his shoulder to Erin. "I wanted to come see Erin."

She couldn't resist that look and placed a hand on his shoulder. "It's all right, Thad. I don't mind you visiting me."

"I mind," Carter barked, but his gaze was focused on Erin, not on Thad. When he shifted his attention back to his son, the anger eased. "I know this isn't like our apartment in New York, but you still have to tell me where you're going, okay?"

"Okay. I *am* sorry, Dad."

Carter's smile was soft, although Erin could still see an edge to the set of his mouth. "It's all right." His gaze glanced off Erin's. "Let's go and let Erin get back to work."

She opened her mouth to protest, but Carter shot her a warning look. She glanced at JD, and from the wrinkle between his brows as he stared at his friend, he was equally puzzled by Carter's attitude toward her. And it was directed at her specifically, of that she had no doubt.

Thad paused at the door. "Thanks for letting me help, Erin. That was great."

"Anytime, Thad."

His smile wasn't nearly as open and cheerful as it had been when he arrived, and that made her mad. He slipped through the door without a response.

Carter cleared his throat. Erin jerked her attention to him.

"I'll make sure he doesn't bother you again," he said.

"He wasn't bothering me."

"Well, it bothers me," Carter said, the words once again sharp.

Erin startled. "I'm sure you don't have to worry about being bothered much, not with that attitude. Want to clue me in on the problem, Mr. Deveraux?"

The words were out of her mouth before she realized she was going to speak them, but she let them stand, unwilling to back down. If this was about the incident on the road Sunday, well, she wasn't going to apologize again. And she wasn't about to lie down and let this man walk all over her.

But apparently, whatever the problem was, *Mr. Deveraux* didn't want to talk about it. Without responding, he turned and walked out, leaving her to stare openmouthed in frustration at the empty space where he'd been standing.

CHAPTER
Seven

"I'm really sorry, Dad."

Thad's words made Carter feel like an absolute asshole. Because he *was* an absolute asshole, but try as he might, he couldn't stop seeing Erin Jenkins as the enemy. She'd had nothing to do with Thad sneaking out. That didn't mean he didn't blame her.

Hell if he knew why, but he did.

His son, however, needed some reassurance. "It's all right." He gripped Thad's thin shoulder, giving him a squeeze but refusing to let go afterward. "You didn't mean to do anything wrong. And I want you to enjoy being here. I just need to know where you're going to be so I don't worry, okay?"

"Okay." With the resilience only a child could show, he began to skip through the fallen leaves, kicking at piles here and there. His childlike wonder at the simplest things never ceased to amaze Carter. For a few moments he let himself absorb that wonder, delight in the joy his son took in the autumn woods.

Until JD cleared his throat beside him.

Here it comes…

"What was all that about?"

"All what?"

JD grunted in irritation. "Don't play stupid with me."

"Not playing stupid," Carter told him. "Just clarifying which part of 'all that' you were wanting to discuss."

"How about the fact that I wasn't sure if you wanted to jump Erin because you thought she'd done something wrong or because you had a hard-on for a totally different reason."

Carter tripped over a broken stick—or at least that's what he told himself. "I didn't have a hard-on."

"Well it's not like I checked, but you could have fooled me." JD paused to step over a fallen log. "Considering there's no way to blame her—legitimately—for Thad going up there, I don't see another explanation."

"Wrong."

Just what JD was wrong about, Carter didn't clarify. He was too busy trying to think up another explanation. Because it couldn't be that he was attracted to Erin. She was nothing like the women he dated—used to date. Right, he wasn't dating right now. He wasn't looking at anyone, much less a woman who seemed to favor braids and flannel and coveralls.

Had that been mud on her boots or something else?

JD started whistling, and Carter fought the urge to punch him in the stomach. Let him find the air to whistle after that. Prick. "I don't have a hard-on for the general contractor."

"Right."

"I don't."

"Okay."

Carter growled low under his breath. "I didn't come here looking for a woman." Especially not that woman. "In fact, after the last disaster Emma sent my way, I've decided not to date at all for a while." And he wasn't changing his mind now. This vacation was about him and his son, not anyone else.

JD huffed out a laugh.

"What?"

"Nothing." The whistling resumed.

Carter stopped in his tracks, jerking around to face JD. "What?"

JD grinned. "Nothing."

Carter narrowed his eyes. JD resumed walking.

Damn it.

"Dad! Come look at this!"

Giving JD a pissed-off side-eye, Carter jogged ahead to see the mushrooms Thad had found growing on a downed log. JD just laughed again, which made it worse. Maybe this was his friend's way of paying him back for the shit Carter gave him while he was navigating the beginning stages of a relationship with Lily.

No, this was nothing like JD and Lily's experience. He wasn't falling for the lady carpenter—if the word *lady* even applied—like JD had fallen for the lady mayor. Nothing whatsoever like that, at all.

Really, he had to get better friends.

They spent the afternoon wandering the woods with JD as a guide—or bait for any bear they ran into, Carter figured. Later JD and Lily invited them to dinner at a restaurant called the Carousel, which immediately had Thad enthralled. Carter let a hot shower wash away the grubbiness of their afternoon before sending Thad in for a shower too. He dressed, set out clothes for their evening, right on the bed where Thad could see them when he came out of the bathroom, then went downstairs and out into the cool October evening to give his business partner, Gavin, a call. It was close to midnight in Scotland, but Gavin was a night owl.

Sure enough, the gruff sound of Gavin's voice, his Scottish accent barely a rumble under the word, answered on the third ring. "Aye?"

"Gavin."

"How ya doin', mate? Nothin's eat ya up yet out there in the woods?"

Carter scoffed. "We're not that far up in the wilderness." He wouldn't admit to Gavin that he'd worried about getting eaten by something until JD reassured them that bears were really all they had to worry about once the weather got as cool as it was now.

He couldn't help a shudder at the thought of snakes.

Gavin conceded nothing; he usually didn't. "It's good for ya to get that boy out in the woods. Concrete and steel aren't the only experiences for a man, yeah?"

Carter sighed. "I know, I know." He felt the same. It was one of the reasons he'd wanted to come here, to give Thad a different experience, one parks in the city definitely couldn't give him. It wasn't shaping up how he'd wanted, however. Thad had been quiet all day. If Carter's own conscience hadn't been nagging at him, his son's disappointment would've done the job plenty well.

"What's goin' on?"

He snapped out of his thoughts. "What do you mean?"

"You're never this quiet unless somethin's on your mind. You're on vacation, you dafty. 'Quiet' shouldn't be describin' your mood, exactly."

Gavin's words only served to ruffle his feathers further. "Maybe I'm just tired."

"Uh-uh. Not buyin' it."

Of course he wasn't. Gavin knew him too well for that. They'd met fresh out of business school at the first firm either of them had worked for, and Carter had become friends with the Scotsman immediately. Now that they'd built their own firm, Gavin was able to travel back and forth between New York and Edinburgh, spending time with his family back home while he handled the international end of their business, but Carter sometimes missed being in the same office. Especially times like these, when he knew JD and Linc would just give him shit if he told them what his brain was chewing on. Gavin tended to be more of a straight shooter. Typical blunt Scot, he said he was.

Might as well spill. "So I might've screwed things up a bit."

"'Might've'? Ya've only been there, wha', two days? How'd ya screw things up already?"

"There's this woman—"

Gavin's groan came through the phone loud and clear. "Of course there is."

"It's not like that."

"Of course it's no'."

Carter's sigh this time was more of a huff. "Can I tell the story or not?"

Gavin grumbled on the other end of the line before acquiescing. "Fine, go 'head."

Carter did. By the end, Gavin wasn't even bothering to hide his laughter.

"The lass got ya to play the fool yourself."

"She didn't make me do anything."

Gavin barked another laugh. "That's no' what I meant and ya know it."

Carter did. Nearly twenty-five years with Gavin as his friend meant he was used to the odd plays on words that Gavin used.

And in this case, his friend was right. He had played the fool.

He groaned.

"Yeah." Gavin almost sounded as smug as JD had this afternoon. Too bad he was halfway across the world, way too far for Carter to get his hands on. "Nothin' for it now but to make amends."

Carter scrubbed his knuckles over his beard. "Yeah, I know."

"Ya knew already; ya just needed me to prod ya along."

Carter snorted at that one. "Don't get too big for your britches, there, friend."

"Hey, I can' help if ya need someone to tell ya what to do."

"I don't need someone to tell me what to do."

"Who's telling you what to do?" Thad asked behind him. "Is that Mom?"

Gavin laughed in his ear. "Good luck explainin' that one."

"Yeah, thanks."

Carter cut off the call and turned to his son. Thad's dark hair, so like his own, was already springing up from its post-shower wetness to curl around his head as he stood at the French doors leading out to the courtyard. Carter's hair did that if he didn't keep it cut close to his head, too. On Thad it was endearing; on a nearly fifty-year-old man whose hair was liberally sprinkled with white? Not so much.

Although he'd had women tell him otherwise.

Shutting off the thought of women, he knelt to straighten the front of Thad's button-down shirt. "You clean up really nice."

"Thanks!" He pulled on his ears, flashing Carter that smile with the gap on the side. "Even cleaned behind them."

"Good man."

He herded Thad back inside, out of the chill air.

"Was that Mom on the phone?"

Carter led the way toward the front door and their coats. "No, it was Gavin."

"Oh." Thad nodded as if it was perfectly sensible that Gavin would be bossing his dad around.

To head off any more of that discussion, he held out Thad's coat for his son to push his arms into. "Did you want to talk to your mom?" He tried to be certain Thad could reach out to Rachel anytime he wanted or needed to. They'd discussed getting him his own phone, but neither Carter nor Rachel wanted to allow the world that kind of access to their son at such a young age.

"Sure!"

"Ready to go?" JD asked. He and Lily descended the stairs, looking like the perfect couple in their semi-formal dress. It struck Carter all over again how perfect Lily was for his friend. Just seeing the happiness on JD's face, the relaxing of the lines around his eyes and mouth that focusing too much on work and not enough on enjoying life had put there, confirmed everything Carter had hoped for when JD had told his friends he and Lily were becoming serious.

"We are." Carter pulled his phone back out of his pocket and used it to gesture Thad toward the door. "Let's get in the car and you can talk to Rachel on our way into town, okay?"

"Okay." Thad pulled the massive front door open with a loud grunt that had the adults laughing, and hurried outside. Sometimes Carter wished he had a tenth of his son's infinite energy.

"That boy could beat us to town if he just kept running," JD said, proving his thoughts were following the same line as Carter's.

"He's like the Energizer Bunny," Lily agreed, grinning.

"We should hurry or he'll have started the car and left us behind before we get outside," Carter joked.

The three adults headed for the door. As Lily stepped through, Carter gave JD's elbow a tug. "Uh, can I ask a favor?"

JD hesitated on his way out. "Of course."

"Can I get Erin's phone number from you?"

A grin split JD's face. "Of course."

Carter gave him a warning look. "Not a word, man."

JD held his hands out, giving the—totally false, Carter knew—impression he would back off. "I didn't say anything." But then he moved through the door, and a whistle drifted back behind him.

Carter rolled his eyes. He was never gonna live this down, was he?

CHAPTER
Eight

A s Erin waited at the podium for her turn to be seated at a table, she smoothed the green sheath of her dress over her hips. She hadn't eaten at the Carousel often, but she knew the upper crust of Black Wolf's Bluff did and she'd pulled out her absolute best for tonight's meeting. Not that she was here for pleasure—she wasn't—but opportunities like this didn't come along often.

A calloused hand cupped her elbow, and she turned to see that her foreman, Wyatt Brown, had arrived. "Hey." A glance behind him didn't reveal the familiar face she was looking for. "Where's Allie?"

Wyatt grimaced. "When I mentioned wanting seafood, she turned green and decided she might ought to stay home."

"Aw." Erin's heart squeezed with a combination of sympathy and envy. "Morning sickness isn't sticking to morning, I take it."

"Doc says it's normal, but..." He shrugged, a look of worried confusion on his face that Erin recognized from working with so many men.

"He's right; it's normal. Doc would tell you if it was anything to be concerned about." Their local GP still did a little bit of everything, including delivering babies, and at close to seventy Erin reckoned he'd seen everything by now. He also wasn't too proud to send his patients to a bigger city for a specialist if they needed it.

Wyatt wiped his hand down his face. "I'll be glad when this stage is over."

Erin opened her mouth to agree but stopped when Marcy called her name from the podium. "Come on with me, you two."

With a smile of sympathy for her foreman, Erin turned to follow Marcy through the restaurant.

The Carousel was one of the most beautiful places Erin had ever visited, a marvel of engineering and luxury. As its name implied, the building was a glass-enclosed circle situated directly on a massive lake off the main thoroughfare bisecting Gatlinburg. The inside decor included gold and crystal and a fully decorated carousel horse at the juncture of each floor-to-ceiling glass panel that surrounded the dining room. Tables covered in sterling white tablecloths topped with gleaming silver, cut-crystal glasses, and sparkling gold chargers waited for the delectable food offered by the top-notch kitchen staff. It was the height of decadence, and Erin found herself wondering what Carter and his precocious little boy would think of it. How would it stack up to the luxuries found in New York City? Would Carter find it lacking? Would Thad delight in the luxurious yet playful atmosphere?

Probably.

The table she and Wyatt were escorted to sat near the center of the room, far from the dusk-filled windows. No need to waste those views on non-paying customers, though Erin didn't think there was a truly bad view in the whole place. The thought of being involved in a second location sent a flutter of excitement through her.

Marcy seated them and returned to her stand. Wyatt whistled low and long. "This place is sure something else, isn't it?"

"It is," she agreed. "And we are up to the job of replicating it. Don't you forget that."

Wyatt had grown by leaps and bounds in both construction skill and leadership ability since she'd taken him on as a young twenty-five-year-old a decade ago. She didn't give the position of foreman to just anyone, not when her clients' wishes were at stake. Wyatt had proven himself time and time again, as he would on this project, she had zero doubt.

He nodded absently, though she could see some concern creeping into his gaze as it roamed the room. No such concern bothered her, and that was the confidence she turned on Jamie Worthington when he stepped up to their table.

"Ms. Jenkins," the owner of the Carousel said, holding out his hand. "It's a pleasure to see such a beautiful addition to my restaurant."

Erin stood and gave the man her hand, willing herself not to blush at the compliment. In his fifties, Jamie Worthington was a big, burly man with the freckled complexion of the true ginger that he was, close-cropped hair and beard gleaming in the golden light of the room. His heavy-set frame should have been intimidating, but the flawless manners that controlled his movements dissipated any concerns a woman might have. Of course, when he bent to kiss the back of her hand, she couldn't help quirking an eyebrow down at him.

Glancing up, she found her gaze caught by a pair of brilliant blue eyes, narrowed on her from across the room. *Carter.* She couldn't quite read his expression from that far away, but something about the look sent a shiver down her spine, a visceral reaction far stronger than anything the kiss on her hand was generating.

Anger? Dislike? It had to be one of the two, not that something else that tingled low in her gut. That was just wrong, considering.

The moment broke when Jamie straightened back to his full height. Erin shook off the strange feeling and forced her attention onto her potential client. "We appreciate you inviting us to talk," she said, retaking her seat.

At the same time, Wyatt stood, cell phone in hand. "Erin." His voice was apologetic, and she knew immediately it was Allie on the line.

"Go see if she's okay," she said, shooing him from the table. As Wyatt hurried across the room toward a quieter spot, she told Jamie, "His wife is pregnant."

Jamie's green eyes softened with understanding. "Always a priority, of course."

"Of course." Fingering the stem of her water glass, she got down to business. "You wanted to talk about a new project?"

"Business before pleasure. A woman after my own heart," he said, signaling a passing waiter. After ordering a drink, he leaned back in his chair, his broad chest no less intimidating for his casual posture. The man's presence, both physical and psychological, filled the space around him. "I understand you're in charge of Black Wolf Resort's construction."

"I am." A chance she was grateful to have. She'd never wanted to be a huge construction outfit. Her aim wasn't so much money as interest. She loved a challenge, she loved making her clients happy, and she loved providing a solid living for the crews who worked for her.

"Surprising for such a small outfit."

He'd done his research, obviously. Good. He wasn't wrong either. Projects like this one normally went to much bigger companies.

"My PR firm is effective," she told him, only half joking. "The mayor of Black Wolf's Bluff drives a hard bargain."

"And JD Lane believed her." Jamie nodded. "When I began looking for a new builder, Lincoln Young told me the story of their new venture. And obviously both Lane's and Mayor Easton's belief in you is paying off."

"I believe it is."

"My research agrees," Jamie said.

Before Erin could say more, Wyatt returned to the table. "I apologize for stepping out. My wife…"

Erin let Wyatt tell his story as she felt her phone vibrate in her purse. Jamie was commiserating, ordering Wyatt a drink from the waiter who had returned with the restaurant owner's desired bourbon, while Erin clicked her screen awake and looked at the waiting text.

> Unknown Caller: I need to apologize to you.

Frowning, she typed a response.

> Erin: Who is this?

Jamie launched into a tale of his ex-wife's journey through first trimester nausea. Erin's phone vibrated again.

> Unknown Caller: Carter.

A jolt went through her body. Her gaze flashed up to meet that sky-blue one again, staring from across the yellow glow that encompassed the crowded dining room. The intensity of that stare did funny things to her stomach.

"I'm Erin's foreman, by the way."

Pay attention, Erin! This is too important to allow distractions.

She shook herself out of her trance. "Wyatt has worked for me for over ten years," she explained. "He's excellent at what he does. As I don't have a business partner and can't be everywhere at once, I rely on his input when it comes to how much our crews can handle."

"Interesting." Jamie asked Wyatt a question, one Erin didn't catch because she'd once again become caught in Carter's stare. She forced herself to drop her attention to her phone.

> Erin: If you want to apologize, I'm right here. Bring it on.

> Carter: Don't want to interrupt.

She wondered if it was not wanting to interrupt or not wanting to be seen begging forgiveness that had him stuck in his seat.

> Carter: Who's the suit?

She nearly choked on her sip of wine.

> Erin: Wow. You just can't stop yourself from putting your foot in your mouth, can you?

She raised a brow at the man and pushed send on the text. Carter glanced down at his phone and paused to read. Before he could respond, Thad bounced up in his chair beside his dad, seeming to use those exclamation points all over again to ask Carter a question. Whatever it was, it took a minute to answer, and then she saw Carter's fingers moving across his phone again. When he looked at her one more time, the nearest corner of his mouth was raised in a half smile that sent an unexpected zing through her.

A vibration had her looking down at her cell.

> Carter: It has to be your fault. It only seems to happen around you.

So it was her fault, was it?

> Erin: That hole you're digging is getting deeper with every text.

She more saw his bark of laughter than heard it from so far away. Still, she realized she was smiling.

Over the jerk.

What was wrong with her?

Whatever game Carter was playing—and it had to be a game—it was best to nip it in the bud before she got any more caught up in it.

> Erin: I'm going back to work now. Bye.

She turned her phone off and laid it aside, putting her full concentration on Jamie and the important conversation going on at her own table. But despite her efforts, some small part of her was still aware, still watching, as Carter and Thad enjoyed their dinner with Lily and JD. Some small voice whispered in the back of her mind, wondering if they'd come by her table on their way out, wondering if Carter liked green. Wondering if Carter was as distracted by her as she was by him.

Why was she distracted by him, of all people? What he'd written wasn't even a true apology, just an "I need to apologize." Not the same thing, and yet her brain was turning it over as the evening wore on, refusing to focus on the topic at hand when a far more interesting one waited just across the room.

CHAPTER
Nine

Things were finally drying out at the job site. Autumn was typically wet in the Tennessee hills, but this season had been even more so than usual, delaying project after project. This week, however, they were finally making steady progress, which Erin was happy to report to JD—via phone, making it less likely to run into any irritating distractions with pretty blue eyes that had zero to do with the job or the weather.

Following the call with her client, Erin spent the morning at the build site, where the crew was finishing the final touches on the steel structure that the rain had put behind schedule. After lunch she started out from the shed, following the drive down the mountain, to touch base with the crew working on the access road. Wyatt waved her over when she reached them, and after going over their progress and addressing concerns, she left him to continue supervising. Walking back up wasn't nearly as quick as walking down, so she took her time, enjoying the clear, cool air and the feeling of accomplishment the day had given her.

It wasn't until halfway back to the shed that she realized she had a shadow following her up the drive.

It started with a quick darting movement caught from the corner of her eye as she turned to watch a hawk ride the air stream down the mountain. Often the predator birds would start at the top and let the wave of air following the contours of the land carry them down into the valley while they surveyed below for hints of prey. Their wings, held out in a still, silent glide, flashed with touches of gold from the afternoon sun, and Erin stopped in the middle of the drive to savor the bird's graceful flight. When the hawk disappeared around a curve in the landscape, she turned to restart her upward trek.

A glimpse of a mop of golden, curly hair, shining against the bark of the thick oak tree it hid behind, snagged her attention at the last moment.

She quickly hid her smile. Not wanting to give up the game, she began to hum, swinging her stocking cap back and forth in her hand, taking her time with each step. The occasional crunch of leaves or snap of a twig followed, but she had to admit the kid was pretty good at keeping his stalking quiet. The knee-high stone wall surrounding the estate was topped with thick cast-iron spindles that provided no cover, but the pillars at regular intervals allowed Thad to slowly advance as Erin passed the gates and continued on toward the building site.

By the time she arrived at the shed, she was winded. Bending over to prop her hands on her knees, she watched through the fall of her bangs as Thad ghosted around her truck, inched his way toward her, and at the last moment, made a final lunge to startle his "unsuspecting" prey.

She jumped at him before he could reach her.

"Arrrrgggghhhh!"

"Aaahhh!"

Thad's surprised shout had Erin clutching her stomach, laughter overwhelming her. Once the boy realized that his target had outwitted him, he too began to laugh, the two of them enjoying the moment until their amusement settled and they were left breathless and grinning at one another.

"You're pretty good at that, you know?" Erin nudged her chin toward the woods. "Not many city boys can be that quiet in the forest, especially not with dry leaves all over the ground."

"I googled 'how to follow someone in the woods without making noise,'" Thad said proudly.

Erin was torn between alarm and more laughter. Maybe she should warn Carter that he had a budding stalker on his hands before the FBI took an interest in his Internet searches. Scarlett had told her once that authors joked about their online queries drawing the wrong kind of attention; she had a feeling Thad's might be equally interesting if this was the way his mind worked. She hoped Carter had invested in family-friendly security software or whatever it was parents used to keep their kids safe on the Internet.

"Well"—she opened the door to the shed—"you seem to be catching on pretty well."

Thad hesitated at the entrance instead of following Erin into her makeshift office. She paused, glancing over her shoulder at him with a raised eyebrow.

"I'm not supposed to bother you."

Erin rolled her eyes. "If you were bothering me, I'd tell you, Thad."

That bright grin flashed across his face. "Okay!"

Deciding it was close enough to the end of the day, she pulled out her latest project and went back to work on sanding the butcher block sections she intended to cut for Claire's stand. After a bit more practice with Thad, she let him take over the palm sander and began the detail work by hand to get the final corners and stubborn sections refined. Carter found them a while later, both happily silent as they focused on their respective tasks. When the creak of the door broke her concentration, Erin glanced up, surprised to see Thad's father in a tight T-shirt that showed every ridge of his abdomen and jogging pants that emphasized the long length of his legs, eyes narrowed on his son as he carefully ran the handheld sander over the board in front of him.

"Thad."

Thad glanced up, caught sight of his dad, and with the care of someone far older, lifted the sander, carefully powered it off, and removed his safety glasses. "Look, Dad! I did it all by myself this time."

"I see that."

Thad seemed to hesitate as Carter moved toward him. "Erin said I wasn't bothering her, promise."

"He's right," Erin put in. "He's not bothering me. It was nice to have someone with strong hands working the sander instead of doing it all by myself."

The mention of his *strong hands* had Thad grinning. The sight of that gap-toothed smile tugged at Erin's heart. She only hoped Carter didn't wipe it away.

Carter took a few moments running his hands over the board Thad had worked on, admiring the smoothness and his son's patience in doing such a time-consuming yet rewarding task. He didn't look at Erin, acknowledge what he'd said last night, didn't even seem aware she was there until he said, "Thad…"

All it took was one look at his father's face and Thad seemed to sense what was coming. "Dad," he said in a comically similar tone, "you said you wouldn't get mad as long as I wasn't bothering Erin."

Carter's mouth twisted, seeming to understand that his son had him in the crosshairs. "I'm not mad."

"You said that last time. I told Uncle JD where I was."

Carter nodded. "You did everything right. But I'd like a chance to talk to Erin on her own. Can you let me do that?"

Thad considered that seriously for a moment. Erin had to hide her smile behind her hand at the adult way Thad was handling this. Handling his father, really. It was hilarious. She bet not a single woman had ever handled Carter so well.

The thought made her choke on a laugh. She thought she'd done a fairly good job hiding it, but Carter's side-eye said otherwise.

Finally Thad nodded. "I can do that." Dusting off his hands and setting his glasses aside, he then moved over to Erin and, without warning, threw himself into her arms. "Thank you for letting me help."

Staring helplessly up at Carter, she gave the boy a hug and patted him on the back. "Anytime, Thad. I like having you work with me."

Carter frowned, but she ignored it. She wasn't going to lie to the boy for his father's comfort.

Only when Thad was headed out the door did Carter speak again. "Go ahead and get cleaned up for dinner, okay?"

"Okay," Thad yelled without looking back.

Long moments of silence stretched out after the little boy's departure. Erin let it ride, unworried. Carter couldn't fault her any more than he had Thad, and whatever he had to say, she hoped it included an apology.

That's not all you were thinking about him saying last night, was it?

She shut that thought down real quick. What she'd thought about Carter in the middle of the night was not something she wanted to acknowledge. She'd woken up hot and sweaty, and not because of the temperature in her house. Best to banish that from her mind forever.

"Erin…"

The fact that that sounded exactly the way he had spoken to Thad had her straightening her spine. "Carter…"

He turned to face her, propping his butt against the work surface Thad had used. She definitely tried to avoid seeing exactly how the move plumped up an already delectable rear.

Carter rubbed at the frown between his brows. Was that

from frustration or irritation?

Knowing she was watching him way too closely, she stood and moved over to her makeshift desk. She hadn't gone through today's mail despite having it piled up. She'd been too busy enjoying her time with Thad. So she pulled out her pocketknife, flicked it open the way she had for years, since she was ten and her father had given her the pretty red knife for her birthday. No pink for her.

"About Thad…"

She picked up an envelope, turned it on its side, and slid the pocketknife into the tiny gap between the envelope and fold. A quick slice forced it open. "What about him?"

"It's important that you send him home whenever he bothers you."

The man was like a dog with a bone. "I'm sure you would prefer that, though I'm not sure why." She shrugged. "But that would be hard to do seeing as how he isn't bothering me."

Carter's frown deepened. Did anyone ever *not* play ball with his ideas? "I don't want him intruding on your work."

"He's not intruding."

Carter waved his hand impatiently, his tone equally so. "You know what I mean."

Now he wasn't the only one getting irritated. "No, I don't. It isn't like Thad is going to be here for months, Carter. He's an inquisitive little boy spending a few days in the woods, and he likes to hang out here. If I'm here, I've told him that's fine. I enjoy his company. He's not annoying me, bothering me, intruding, or whatever other verb you want to use to describe it. Stop worrying and let the kid be."

"The kid doesn't need to get attached to someone he's never going to see again."

She jerked the knife through the envelope of a bank statement, removed the paper from inside, and tried to keep her rising emotion out of her voice. "If JD continues to live here

65

with Lily, and you continue to be friends with him, likely you'll see me another time or two. I don't think being friends with someone for a few days is going to permanently traumatize your son."

"That's my decision to make!"

She jerked, and without warning the pocketknife slipped in her hands, missing the envelope she was aiming for and cutting right across her palm. "Ow! Shit!"

Carter's curse echoed her own. Erin barely noticed as she dropped the envelope and knife onto her desk and gripped her wrist tight. Christ, that stung.

Silence filled the shed. Erin sucked in a breath, let go of her wrist, and dug in her pocket for a handkerchief—something else her father had taught her to carry.

"Here, let me see."

A glance at Carter's face showed his skin white as a sheet, eyes fixed and staring at her wrist as he crossed the room.

"You're bleeding."

"Mm." She applied the bandanna to the thin but deeper-than-she'd-like slice. "It's no big deal."

"You're bleeding."

This time the words were grated through his teeth. Erin pressed on the cut and grated out her own, "Don't worry about it."

Carter rolled his eyes at that. "Where's your first-aid kit?"

Sweeping the shed with a look, Erin saw the clear plastic box on the workbench near the door. "Over there."

Carter's gaze landed on it, and he had it up and over to her desk in a heartbeat. "Sit."

She pressed the kerchief harder against her skin, then hissed when the cut stung. "Do you ever do anything but bark orders and irritate people?"

He rolled his eyes. The hand not holding the kit came up, planted itself in the middle of her chest, and pressed her backward. "Sit."

CHAPTER

Ten

G uess she had no choice. She plopped into the metal chair behind her, giving Carter her most annoyed look. He ignored it and opened the kit.

"Why is a letter opener sharp enough to cut you?" he asked as he rummaged through the kit's contents.

"It's not a letter opener. It's a pocketknife."

"Why is a pocketknife that sharp?" He stepped close, his heat reaching her as he began organizing bandages and ointment and alcohol wipes on her work desk, in order of use. The realization amused Erin, and she answered him absently.

"Because what use is a knife if you don't keep it sharp?"

Carter froze, his astonished gaze locking with hers before he shook his head and went back to what he was doing. "Right, not Kansas," he muttered.

The reference to *The Wizard of Oz* made her chuckle. "If you think this is Kansas, you've got bigger problems than a little cut."

Carter huffed again. He reached for her, taking over the pressing of the hankie as he extended her arm to bring it closer to himself. Again with the propping of his butt on the edge of the makeshift desk. She was going to have dreams about that butt; she just knew it.

The front wasn't bad either.

Just stop looking! She didn't want to have dreams about anything attached to an annoying jackass. A too-handsome-to-ignore jackass, but a jackass nonetheless.

She hadn't realized she was pulling back on her hand until Carter spoke again. "Stop that."

"Sorry." Relaxing her arm beneath his touch was an act of will.

"I can't believe you cut yourself with a knife."

Familiar irritation roughened his voice. Was this man ever *not* going to be irritated with her?

"Believe me, Carter, I've cut myself with a lot worse." Construction wasn't a delicate job. She'd had more stitches than she could remember.

He scowled; that was the only way to describe the fierce expression that appeared on his face. "You really should be more careful then."

"You really shouldn't argue with me when I'm holding a knife," she countered.

He lifted the hankie, grunted, replaced the cloth, then reached for the alcohol wipes. Tearing a couple of the tiny packets open with his teeth, he mumbled, "This might hurt."

She snorted, hoping the sound kept him from noticing the way her gaze fixated on his mouth. It was just right, not too full and not too thin. Just enough of a pout to make kissing good, she bet.

Dragging her focus away from his lips—which she definitely shouldn't be noticing—she zeroed in on Carter's eyes. The look they held was half determination, half apology. Did he look like that when he was cleaning Thad's cuts? She imagined he did. He was obviously a good dad. When he bent his head over her hand, she couldn't help but notice that his short, dark-blond hair was growing out a little, the ends beginning to show hints of the same soft curls his son's head sported. Her fingers spasmed, the urge to touch those curls strong. Thankfully the alcohol hit her cut about the same time, and she hissed, barely keeping from letting loose a few choice expletives.

"Easy, there."

Warm breath hit her skin as Carter bent farther to blow gently on the cut, dissipating the sting. Erin sucked in a breath, her lungs filling with the faint dusty scent of the shed and something spicy, like cedar. *Carter.* She closed her eyes and tried not to notice that scent, the strength of the fingers touching her, the heat of his body so close. She fought the urge to shift in her seat and lost.

This was dangerous.

She flicked her eyes open. "You know, you never did apologize." The words were the slightest bit strained, but she was proud of herself for getting them out. "Now might be a good time for that."

"I did apologize." A couple rubs of the wipes across her cut was accompanied by more puffs of air to relieve the pain. "I texted you an apology."

His prevaricating amused her; why, she wasn't sure. Because seeing Carter on edge gave her some sense of control, probably.

"You texted me that you needed to apologize. That's not an actual apology."

"Same thing," he bit out, sounding remarkably like his ten-year-old son.

She chuckled. "Is it?" Ducking her head, she forced Carter to meet her gaze. "Would you let Thad get away with that?" she asked, brow lifted.

Frustrated realization flashed in Carter's eyes. "You know I wouldn't."

The words sounded like they were being dragged out totally against his will. She didn't bother to hide her satisfaction. Carter, face still so close to hers, dropped his gaze to her smiling mouth.

Erin cleared her suddenly thick throat. "Then I won't let you get away with it either."

"Get away with what?"

The words were distracted, husky, his gaze still on her mouth.

"Not apologizing."

The teasing tone had somehow disappeared from her words. In fact, the words barely made it out, her lips feeling too full under Carter's intense focus.

He nodded absently. "I'm sorry I was abrupt with you when we first met."

"Abrupt?"

His eyes met hers. "Uh-huh."

He was staring. Why was he staring? She didn't know what he saw in her gaze, but whatever it was had his own eyes darkening, and for once it wasn't irritation she read in his expression. It was…

It took her a moment, maybe because it had been so long since she'd seen that look in a man's eyes when his attention was on her, but the flare of hunger had a similar spark igniting in her core. Her throat closed completely, almost choking her.

Damn.

Carter's grip on her arm tightened, pulling her closer. Erin went, though she wasn't certain she should. The spell those eyes held her in prevailed, however, and she inched closer and closer, arguing with herself the whole way.

Then Carter's breath hit her lips—warm, sweet like mint. So enticing. Her gaze dropped to his mouth.

At the last moment, before both of them were lost, she saw those tempting lips dip into a frown, and then he was taking her mouth in a hungry kiss that ignited the sparks in her belly to a roaring flame, just as she'd known it would. There was no easing in, no hesitation in Carter's touch. Only taking, and Erin knew in that moment that she'd been fooling herself. She wasn't uncertain—she wanted him, definitely, defiantly, whether she should or not. Wanted his kiss, his touch. It didn't make sense, not with the animosity between them, but in that moment she didn't care.

And Carter didn't seem to either. His hands circled her neck, his thumbs firmly guiding her head as his tongue breeched her lips. He devoured her—there was no other word for it. His lips, his tongue, his scent and the heat of his body as he pushed her back in the chair took her over completely. A moan escaped him as she returned lick for lick, thrust for thrust, savoring the taste of man and heat and desire. It was like her skin filled out the second his mouth met hers, making her intensely aware of herself as a woman, of Carter as a man, of all the possibilities between them. Possibilities she wanted to explore.

And then Carter jerked back and the possibilities fizzled like ash in the wake of the fire that had consumed them.

"I—" Carter shook his head as if emerging from a daze. "I apologize. I shouldn't have done that."

He dropped her hand, and Erin yelped as it hit his knee.

"Shit!" He jumped up, knocked her hand with his hip, then backed quickly away. "I'm sorry."

She growled. "Be still and stop being an ass, Carter."

He froze, obviously startled. She wasn't sure what reaction she expected next, but it definitely wasn't deep masculine laughter. The sound restarted the tingles in her belly.

"I am being an ass, aren't I?"

She reached for the antibiotic ointment on her desk. "You most definitely are."

"Here, let me do that." Retracing his steps, Carter took the ointment out of her hand, applied it carefully, then added a bandage to her palm. "There."

"That whole procedure took far longer than it had to."

Because it had been interrupted with an apology and a kiss. The hottest kiss she'd had in...well, maybe since Stephen had died.

No, not maybe. Definitely.

The thought of her husband brought a brief flicker of sadness, but Erin pushed it away. Stephen would want her to be happy. Worry over his reaction had never kept her from dating; it was the refusal to accept anything less than she'd had with him that had kept her single all these years. She'd known true passion; she wouldn't settle for a cheap copy.

Which made her reaction to Carter even more confusing.

"I don't think I've ever apologized to anyone more than I've had to with you," Carter said, his grin wry when she glanced up at him.

"You've never apologized to anyone more than once? I find that hard to believe."

He rolled those pretty blue eyes. "I'm sorry, Erin."

She grinned. "Better." Standing brought her a little too close for comfort to his hard body, but she did it anyway. "Even better would be if you stopped doing things you needed to apologize for."

"I would if you'd stop getting to me."

Something feminine inside her preened at his admission—not that she'd share that with anyone anytime soon. She didn't even want to share it with herself. This whole thing was ridiculous. Weird. And yet she couldn't deny that just being near this man brought her alive in a way she hadn't experienced in a long, long time. Yes, sometimes that "life" was irritation, but not always.

Example a: the butterflies that still fluttered in places she really shouldn't be thinking about right now. She sucked in a breath, filling her lungs with the scent of him once more.

No, definitely not always.

"It's hard to stop when I don't know how I'm getting to you."

"How are you not?" Carter shook his head. From the corner of her eye she saw his hand rise, squeeze shut, then drop back to his side. "I don't know how you do it either; just that you do."

"I'll keep that in mind from now on."

"Do." This time his hand rose all the way, his fingers brushing tendrils of her hair back behind her ear. "Being close to you is dangerous."

"Probably shouldn't have admitted that," she murmured. It was the same thought she'd had earlier, but she found it gratifying that she wasn't the only one to have it.

Definitely not something he needed to know.

Carter cleared his throat, stepping away from her. As she watched, he retreated to the door. Before he could disappear, she found herself calling out.

"Carter."

He turned. "Yeah?"

Her mind blanked for a moment, staring into eyes that were far too distracting. And then she remembered her thought and smirked. "I accept your apology."

CHAPTER
Eleven

Thursday started out quietly. Carter took care of some business early; then he and Thad spent the rest of the morning working up an appetite with a hike in the woods. There really was nothing like autumn in the Smoky Mountains. The cool mountain air warmed as they wandered among the trees and scaled over the craggy rocks— well, Thad did more scaling than Carter did. Brilliant colors decorated the trees even as the crisp crackle of fallen leaves crunched beneath their feet. Carter basked in the time spent with Thad totally away from the stresses of home and the demands of their life back in New York, watching his son blossom in a whole new environment. There was nothing better than that.

By the time they returned to the house, they were more than ready for a brunch of omelets and toast. Carter cooked, and the smell of bacon frying lured JD to join them. They devoured the food in half the time it took to make it, and Carter and JD were starting on cleanup when Lily walked into the kitchen, her phone to her ear and a disgruntled look on her face.

"No, Evan, it's fine. Just hold him off long enough for me

to get down there, okay?" Murmurs came through the cell as she passed Carter on the way to the fridge. "I told you it's fine. I'll figure things out. Okay. See you in a few."

JD frowned from the sink where he was elbow-deep in suds. "Everything okay."

Lily retrieved a bottle of water from the fridge. "Dwayne Prescott is demanding to see me 'right this damn minute.'" Her sigh seemed to come from her toes. "You know how he is —every minute, the sky is falling and it's my fault."

JD grunted his opinion of that. "Thank God he's not running for city council again. Come January he'll be out of your hair."

"That day can't come soon enough." Lily added the water to her already full arms as she joined JD at the sink. "But right now he is in my hair, and I need to get to the office asap. Can you run to pick Erin up? She ran back to the house to help Scott with something and now her truck won't start. I would go, but…"

The mention of Erin sent a frisson of awareness down Carter's spine that he tried hard to ignore, just like he'd been trying to ignore the remembered feel of her mouth since last night. Unfortunately he hadn't succeeded, even in his dreams. He hadn't woken up with a hard-on like that in a very long time.

Not that he was thinking about it now, in the middle of the kitchen with Lily and JD and his son right there. Definitely not.

JD rinsed his hands. "I've got a conference call in fifteen minutes that I can't miss." He grabbed a towel to dry off. "Hey, maybe Carter and Thad can go pick her up. Thad might enjoy seeing the animals at the farm."

Carter gave his best friend a dirty look. Oh, he knew it was logical for him to go, but JD knew as well as he did that having him and Erin in such close proximity was putting a match to flame.

Well maybe JD didn't know as well as Carter did, since he didn't know about the kiss last night. Nobody knew about the kiss last night except for him. In fact, he wished *he* didn't know about the kiss last night.

Denial's not doing you any good, my man.

He ran a heavy hand over his forehead.

Still, he wasn't going to offer. He should avoid being around Erin as much as possible.

"Yay," Thad said, jumping up from the table. "I'll go get my shoes back on."

Carter squeezed his eyes shut. Great.

Opening his eyes, he couldn't hold back a, "Guess that decides that."

He'd hoped the fact that the words were said against the rim of his abruptly raised coffee cup might hide them, but JD's chuckle said otherwise. "Yes, I believe it does." JD's glee made the urge to punch him rise up, causing Carter's fingers to twitch, especially when JD moved toward the cabinets. "Here, take that coffee to go."

And that's how he found himself on the road heading east out of Black Wolf's Bluff, directions to Erin's house on the seat beside him. Lily had insisted on giving him written instructions, claiming the GPS was unreliable the farther out you got from town. JD's final dig as he walked out the door was still ringing in his ears:

"Don't let Willard see you or he'll get jealous."

Lily had given her fiancé a startled look before laughing her way out the door. Carter just wanted to know who the hell Willard was. Erin's boyfriend? Did she have a boyfriend? No one had said she did, but then he remembered the man next to her at the Carousel the other night and a surge of something uncomfortably like jealousy rose into his throat. Not that there was any need to be jealous—it was one kiss, that was all. It hadn't meant anything more than impulse. Frustration run amok.

So why are your knuckles turning white from your death grip on the steering wheel?

Narrowing his eyes at the voice in his head, he consciously relaxed his grip and forced his focus to the road curving back and forth before him. They'd followed Main Street through town and out the opposite side, where the road twisted and turned through the foothills in a way that thankfully demanded his attention. He passed the instructions back to Thad, allowing his son to decipher Lily's writing and direct their path, a task Thad gave all due attention.

Almost half an hour later they topped a rise to discover a vast meadow spread out before them. The flat plain was nestled between two ridges topped with a color kaleidoscope of fall trees. The road dropped into the valley and curved around the southern edge, where Carter passed a turnoff to a farm dominated by a large white house on a rise surrounded by various outbuildings. CARDINAL FARMS, the sign over the driveway said. The next drive they passed led to a massive red barn surrounded by horses, goats, a couple of cows, some geese, and even a donkey.

The third turnoff was Erin's house, a quaint cottage with a couple of outbuildings and a fence that divided her yard from the barnyard. Carter admired the neatness of her home, though he'd expected nothing less from the sassy general contractor. She had order and control written all over her. Except last night. After he'd kissed her, she'd been flush with desire, her eyes soft and hazy—until reality had returned, for both of them.

Yeah, he definitely needed to stop thinking about that.

He stopped the SUV a few feet from the porch and turned it off. Just as he reached for the door handle, a blue streak rounded the far corner of the house and zoomed toward them. It took a moment for his brain to register what his eyes were actually seeing: a massive peacock, his feathers spread wide like the biggest fan Carter had ever seen, speeding across the yard.

Thad unhooked himself from his seat belt in the back and got up to poke his head between the front seats. "Look at that, Dad! A peacock!"

"A very big peacock," Carter agreed. Massive, in fact. He'd known the birds were big, but somehow knowing had not prepared him for the confrontation of the enormous animal charging toward his vehicle.

The bird ran right up to the front of the SUV, his head easily as high as the hood, and stared with beady eyes at the two of them through the windshield. Somehow Carter got the impression they were being assessed as a threat. The thought was confirmed when the animal stalked its way around to the passenger side of the vehicle and began to peck at the window.

Pop. Pop. Pop.

"Uh, Dad?"

Caaaaaaaw! The peacock's shrill cry filled the air, a screeching sound that had Carter jerking back.

Caaaaaaaw! Pop. Pop. Pop. Caaaaaaaw!

He reached for his phone, part of his brain wondering why he was moving so slowly. It wasn't as if a sudden movement was going to make this crazy—and Carter was pretty sure it was crazy—bird any angrier.

"Let's just see where Erin is," he told Thad.

"Uh-huh."

He pulled up his texts and scrolled to find Erin's number, keeping the bird in his peripheral vision.

Clicking on Erin's name distracted Thad from his fascination with the peacock. "Do you have Erin's phone number?"

Oops. "Uh, yeah. JD gave it to me." Thad didn't need to know that he'd had it awhile instead of just getting it this morning.

He shot Erin a quick text.

Carter: What the heck is wrong with this
bird?

It took a moment, but then he saw the three bouncing dots
as Erin replied.

Erin: Don't get out of the car! Wait for me.

Well that didn't sound good. He gave the still-pecking,
crying bird another wary look. "Erin says to wait in the car,"
he told Thad.

Thad watched carefully as the peacock began a slow circle
of the SUV. "Prolly a good idea," he said.

A minute later the front door of the cottage opened, and
Erin stomped out onto the porch. He could hear her boots
banging on the wood, and the look on her face— He
would've laughed if he wasn't slightly terrified of what the
damn bird was going to do to her, a fear that got stronger
when the peacock immediately raised its head and turned
toward her. The fear turned to laughter when the bird ran, its
feathers still in a full-body spread but wobbling uncontrol-
lably back and forth, body waddling like a duck on steroids,
toward its owner. Thad burst out laughing too, clutching his
belly as the bird took flight, bypassing the stairs by a couple
of feet to get to Erin. And then it put its head down and
pushed its body against Erin's leg, rattling its feathers as if
shaking off water.

"What's it doing?" Thad asked.

"I'm not sure." The animal almost reminded him of a cat
claiming its owner, except it wasn't rubbing along Erin's leg.
More like trying to knock her over. "We'll ask Erin when it's
safe to get out."

They waited while Erin put what looked like some bird
seed in a bowl at one end of the porch. When the peacock

turned his attention to the food, Erin hurried down the steps toward the SUV.

"Sorry about that," she said, a bit breathless as she pulled herself into the truck. "Willard is a bit possessive."

Willard?

It was Thad who asked, echoing Carter's thoughts.

"Yeah." She shook her head, her thick ponytail swinging back and forth against her shoulders. "He belongs to my father-in-law, but he's decided for some reason that he's in love with me. Peacocks are highly territorial."

The pieces gradually snapped together in Carter's mind— Willard, possessive, boyfriend. When they finally made sense, he couldn't hold back a groan.

"What?" Erin asked, eyeing him.

"JD warned us about Willard."

Thad piped up. "He didn't say he was a bird, though."

No, no he didn't. Bastard.

In an effort to avoid further discussion—and avoid the sense of Erin's heat, her scent and energy taking over the small space between them—Carter threw over his shoulder, "Buckle up, bud." When he glanced back to be sure his son was complying, he noticed a smirk on Erin's face. He wasn't about to ask what that was for—he was too sure he already knew.

Wait, had she said Willard belonged to her *father-in-law*?

As he backed down the driveway, he told himself not to ask. It was bad enough she knew he'd thought Willard was human. He didn't need to make things worse by asking about a father-in-law.

And yet…

"You said he belongs to your father-in-law?"

Idiot.

But Erin didn't slap back with a sassy reply. Instead she gestured toward the barn. "My in-laws own Cardinal Farms. Willard just refuses to stay over there."

In-laws? He cleared his throat.

"My husband worked with his dad on the farm until his death a few years ago," Erin explained without him having to ask. And really, it made him an asshole that the tension drained from his body at the word *death*, didn't it? Not that he was happy her husband had died; he wasn't. He was just glad there wasn't a husband.

Christ. No, he wasn't glad. He wasn't anything when it came to Erin. Whether or not she had a husband wasn't any of his business, nor was how good she smelled or how mesmerizing her eyes were, especially when the green lit with sparks of temper. He needed to start actually believing that instead of simply repeating it in his head.

As he pulled even with the farmhouse, a small figure darted out into the road. Erin groaned as Carter brought the SUV to a halt.

Thad leaned as far forward as his seat belt would allow him. "Is that a calf?"

"It is." She unlocked her seat belt. "How do you feel about meeting him?" she asked Thad. "We have to catch him first."

Thad bounced in his seat. "Let's go."

Carter put the SUV in park and gave his son a nod. "Have fun."

While Thad wrestled himself out of his seat, Erin gave Carter a sly look. "Not joining us?"

Run around the road trying to catch an animal with two more legs and a lot less weight than him? Sounded like a job for a young'un, as they say. "Not on your life."

CHAPTER

Twelve

Thursday was typically pub night according to JD, though tonight would be cut short due to everyone pitching in to set up for the town's harvest festival this weekend. JD had assured him it was okay to bring Thad, so this time it was the four of them—JD, Carter, Thad, and Erin—piled into the SUV to head back into town at dusk.

Erin had showered at the house. The scent of her damp hair and the fresh, clean smell of the soap she'd used reached him in the driver's seat and sent frissons of awareness down his spine, tingling in places he really wanted to ignore, especially with his son in the car. And yet he was also getting used to it. It seemed like that heightened awareness was now a given anytime he and Erin were in the same room. Not like he had to do anything about it.

Keep telling yourself that, man.

The town square was a bustling hive of activity as he pulled the SUV into a parking space in front of the town bakery, Gimme Sugar. The owner, Claire, was dating his friend Lincoln long distance, but Carter and Thad had not gotten around to meeting her yet this trip. From what Linc said, she was a handful—probably exactly what his friend needed. Too many women bowed down to Linc's looks and his celebrity. From what JD had mentioned to Carter, Claire had no such illusions about their friend, and no qualms about standing up to him when necessary.

"Have you gotten to visit the bakery?" Erin asked Thad in the back seat where the two were unbuckling their seat belts.

"Not yet."

"Let's stop in. We have a few minutes before we have to meet everyone for dinner."

"Great idea," JD said, stepping out of the SUV. "You guys say hi to Claire while I go on over to the Drunken Otter and make sure we have tables saved. Everything's hopping tonight."

JD headed toward the square, and Erin and Thad joined Carter on the sidewalk.

"Why is the otter drunk?"

Erin smirked. "Because it's Irish."

Carter choked on a laugh. "More like an Irish tradition." He had no idea if that was true or not, but he didn't want Thad trying to figure out all night how an otter got drunk.

Thad contemplated that as they headed for the bakery. "To have drunk otters?"

Erin was full-on laughing by now, with no attempt to hide it. When she met his eyes, he mouthed, *Thanks.*

You're welcome, she mouthed back.

"No," he said to Thad. "To name their pubs 'drunken' something. Drunken Otter, Drunken… Goat. Drunken…" He came up blank, and a glance at Erin said she wasn't going to help. "Anyway, you get the idea."

Thank goodness Thad seemed to buy it.

The sidewalk was full of people carrying supplies back and forth, already working on the booths for the weekend festival. Bypassing an overall-clad man carrying buckets of dirt—weird—they made their way into the town bakery. Carter held the door for Thad and Erin to enter the store.

Erin leaned in as she passed. "Good one, Dad," she mumbled.

He hmphed in reply.

Other than the fact that Linc's girlfriend owned Gimme Sugar, Carter knew very little about the store, but one step in was all it took to know he liked it. The scent of brown butter and sugar filled his nose as he walked inside. A quick glance showed him a mix of everything from simple cookies to designer cakes lining the walls and shelves. Gimme Sugar was doing a brisk business despite the late hour, likely due to the heavy traffic in town and whatever was going on at the coffee shop next door, from which loud music and raucous laughter was emanating.

Erin led them up to the counter.

"Claire." The affection in her voice tugged at Carter, reminding him of the relationship between himself and his "adopted" brothers. He and JD and Linc were as close as family, and in the past few years Gavin had also become an integral part of his life. It seemed to him that Erin and Lily and Claire shared a similar bond.

"Who do we have here?" A lovely dark-haired woman, her warm brown skin dusted with flour along one cheek, gave them a big smile. "Am I finally getting to meet the infamous Thad?"

Thad's giggle was inherently childlike, a sound that never failed to tug at Carter's heartstrings. "That's me!"

Claire leaned over the counter to offer Thad her hand. "Well, I'm so glad to have you here." She raised pretty brown eyes to Carter. "And you."

Carter shook the woman's hand. "Hello, Claire."

Thad was staring around the store. "Do you have any sugar-free marshmallows?"

Thad hadn't forgotten. Sometimes Carter wondered what he'd done to be made caretaker to the kind soul Thad possessed.

"I don't think I have any on hand," Claire was saying. "I do have regular ones in the back. They're shaped like pumpkins. Would you like one?"

"Dad can't have those." Thad's disappointment was obvious.

Claire glanced up at him. Carter shrugged. "I'm diabetic." He squeezed Thad's shoulder. "But you can have one, bud."

"We were hoping to roast marshmallows," Thad explained.

Claire's bright smile made a reappearance. "Well, I can certainly make you some. And maybe some other goodies to go along with them. What night are y'all having a fire?"

"JD said something about Saturday after the festival."

"Awesome." Claire gestured toward a display case holding various delicacies. "Let's talk about what you like, Thad."

While the two navigated the wonders of the display case, Carter wandered around the room, conveniently ending up where Erin stood in front of the individually wrapped peanut butter pumpkins coated in chocolate.

She kept her head down. "Diabetic, huh? This place must be a nightmare."

Carter chuckled. "When I was a kid, yeah. But I was diagnosed at twelve, so I'm kind of used to it. It's not that I can't have any sugar, just that I have to be really careful. Most of the time it's just not worth it." He threw a glance over his shoulder. "Thad is pretty enthusiastic about sharing treats with me, so we've had to have long discussions about food and carbs and balance. Luckily he gets it, and it's definitely helped him at school when one of his friends was diagnosed as Type 1 as well."

"And here I thought you were just a hyper-vigilante parent who refuses to allow their kids to have sugar."

Was that so? "Glad to know you were wrong?"

"Maybe." Her grin was sly and half hidden as she turned

back toward the goodies in front of her. It shouldn't make him feel warm inside, having Erin say something nice about him —however halfhearted—but he had to admit it did. He was having to admit a lot of things around Erin; he just had no idea what to do about it all.

After letting Thad pick out a couple of chocolate truffles to have before bedtime, and assuring Claire they'd save her a seat, they made their way over to the Drunken Otter. Similar to the bakery, Carter liked the atmosphere of the pub immediately. The place was a sort of cross between a restaurant and bar, with a dance floor and room for a band. Lily was waiting, and she and JD had gathered several tables together in the middle of the room for what she assured Carter would be a big group. Sure enough, the chairs slowly filled up with Lily and JD's friends, including a blonde who introduced herself as a romance author, and the couple who would watch Thad later tonight while Carter stayed to help out—Evan, Lily's assistant, and his fiancée, Alana. Carter got great vibes from them immediately, and when Alana plopped into the seat next to Thad and began a conversation as if they'd known each other forever, Carter could see why Lily had recommended them.

Feeling a rumble in his midsection, he picked up a menu from the stand in the middle of the table. "So what's good?"

The mention of food brought Thad's attention around as well, so much so that he was practically bouncing in his seat. Both of their appetites had been healthy since they'd been spending so much time in the clean mountain air.

JD pulled the menu out of Carter's hands. "Wings."

"Wings!" Thad clapped.

"Wings, huh?" Carter gave his friend a wry smile. "Somehow I've never equated the words 'Irish pub' and 'wings.' Shepherd's pie, maybe, but wings?"

The entire table erupted with loud groans and moans and

ecstatic sighs, extolling the virtues of the wings available at the Drunken Otter.

JD grinned. "Trust me, dude, you want the wings."

He raised an eyebrow. "Okay, wings it is."

Turned out JD—and the rest of the crowd gathered around them—wasn't wrong. The owner, Clayton, had apparently trained in Texas as well as Ireland, because his wings were out of this world. Before dinner was over, Thad and Carter both had a pile of bones in front of them that would rival the remains of the biggest carnivores to ever walk the Earth. Thad had added spicy fries to his meal (and Carter had insisted on a milk to wash down that spice). For Carter it was the local brew, which had just the right kick to it. The meal was filled out with conversation and laughter, that feeling of camaraderie that only comes with a group of like-minded, longtime friends.

When the food was decimated, Evan and Alana stood, preparing to take Thad back to the mansion. "I brought a game," Alana admitted, her grin shy and the slightest bit crooked. "My niece and nephew really love it, and they stomp all over me every time we play. Have you ever heard of Exploding Kittens?"

"Has he ever heard of it?" Carter's question was definitely rhetorical. "Not only has he heard of it, but he stomps on me regularly too."

"Uh-oh!" Evan laughed. "I'm quaking in my boots now."

Thad grinned up at him. "You should be!"

"Which cat is your favorite?" Alana asked.

"Hairy Potato Cat!" Thad cried.

"Mine's Tacocat."

Thad's grin dimmed as he turned back to me. "I just remembered, I didn't get enough chocolates for Evan and Alana."

"That's okay," Claire said from across the table. "I added in a few of their favorites to go along with yours."

"Awesome!"

Alana held out her hand. "Let's go then."

The hug Thad gave him before heading out the door made Carter's heart feel like mush. He watched until the trio was well across the town square, Thad with one hand in Alana's as they crossed the street, looking as if he was protecting her instead of the other way around. Only when they reached Evan's car did Carter drain the last of the water that had accompanied his single beer and then turn to Erin. "Well, ready to put me to work?"

"Is that even a question?"

CHAPTER
Thirteen

A ccording to Lily, Erin volunteered every year to head the construction portion of the setup for the town's annual harvest festival. As their large group of adults left the pub behind, she assigned them to various booths and parts of downtown to help out. Carter and JD were led toward the west side of the square. As they passed the post office, Carter noticed an elderly woman, her hair an eye-catching fluorescent yellow, setting up a series of corn-hole games whose boards were each painted with a cartoon monster. Shelves of prizes had been erected against the front facade of the post office, awaiting the winners of the games. It wasn't so much the hair that made him do a double take as it was what the woman held at the end of the leash attached to her wrist: a massive orange and white striped tabby. The cat eyed their group as they approached on the sidewalk, looking like a king eyeing his peons.

JD noticed his distraction and called out, "Hello, Lou! How is Snookums tonight?"

"Snookums?" Carter asked out of the side of his mouth.

"What else would he be named?"

Carter laughed when JD got caught up discussing

Snookums's latest vet visit while Erin dragged Carter away. When they arrived at the First Baptist Church behind the post office, Carter was a bit relieved to see the couple she introduced him to was a bit less eccentric and incredibly kind. Mr. and Mrs. Gibson were well into their seventies and reminded him somewhat of his own grandparents when they'd been alive.

"For years we owned a sweets shop across town," Mrs. Gibson told him, her kind smile gleaming against wrinkled black skin. "That was before that lovely young woman, Claire, started Gimme Sugar. Got to the point where it was time for us to retire, you know, but everyone loved our caramel apples, and even if we're gettin' on in years, we love doing things like this for the kids, don't we?" She waved a hand to her husband.

"Course we do." Mr. Gibson said from his seat near the front of the booth, his cane leaning against the side of his leg as he sorted the signs for the various flavors of caramel apples they offered.

"I'm certain the kids appreciate it." Carter lightly tapped a nail into place, putting the shelves together to hold the trays of goodies for tomorrow night. As he worked, he watched Mrs. Gibson tack the signs her husband handed her to the trays that would hold each flavor of apple: cookies and cream, pecan rolled, chocolate dipped, s'mores, even one titled *margarita.* "My mouth is watering just thinking about all of those."

"Well drop on by tomorrow and we'll give you a taste, you and your boy," Mr. Gibson assured him.

JD finally managed to untangle himself from the post-mistress, and he and Carter erected the tent that would provide shade for the Gibsons and their sweets. Once the tables were moved into position and chairs added, including a comfortable rocker on a thin carpet out front where Mrs. Gibson would read spooky tales to the children on the hour, the two men went looking for their next assignment, heading toward the old Victorian off the south side of the square where Erin was supposed to be setting up the town haunted house. Along the way, JD was pulled aside by Lily to help unload a trailer of hay bales. From the looks of the buckets of mums and various other decorations, Carter figured the bales would be the foundation for photo-taking areas in front of the courthouse.

The credit union next to the Drunken Otter was setting up bouncy houses in their parking lot. The crew gave him a wave as he walked by, as friendly as everyone else he'd met in town. Everyone except Erin, at least. Too bad that sassy mouth turned him on instead of turning him off.

At the corner he made a right and walked down two lots to find an old Victorian-era building that needed little in the way of decoration to be perfect for a haunted house. The white paint was chipped and peeling in places, the green roof covered in dark spots where the trees scraping over it had piled their fallen leaves. The fish-scale siding along the upper peaks of the house were still present, as was the elaborate molding along the wraparound porch and the dark eyes of the windows staring out onto the street. As Carter watched, lights flickered inside, shining in the dusk, adding to the impression of eyes. He imagined the place in bright sunlight instead of dark, with sunny flowers instead of the spooky cemetery planted in the front yard, and got a small taste of what he thought it must have looked like a couple hundred years ago.

Walking up the front steps, he realized that despite the aura of neglect, the house was solid. The steps didn't creak or give beneath his feet, and the newel post was strong beneath his hand. He crossed the porch, noting the cartoon style Erin had chosen for what JD had explained was more "fun" haunted house than scary. This attraction was intended for younger children, and each room inside had been matched to a Dr. Seuss–style story to entertain the groups as they were led throughout the house. Apparently this was a regular feature at the harvest festival, one JD said Erin took special interest in and one the children of the town looked forward to every year.

"There you are. Where's your sidekick?" Erin asked as he pushed through the door.

"Got sidetracked by his fiancée." He glanced around the foyer, draped in spiderwebs and shadows thrown by spooky lighting.

"Don't look up," Erin whispered as she passed by. So of course he did. Hanging from the two-story-high ceiling was a massive spider, its eyes glowing in the darkness. He grinned when he spotted the glow-in-the-dark bow tie around its neck.

"Cute."

She smiled over her shoulder.

He followed her into the room to his right. A witch's workroom waited inside, complete with smoking cauldron and eyes of newt blinking inside jars on the shelves. The stories might be a little young for him, but Carter couldn't wait to see Thad's reactions to the decorations here.

Erin led him through a cavern that was home to a massive basilisk (and its hundred babies) and a mad scientist's lair complete with a variety of experimental beakers foaming in supernatural colors and a few animals whose characteristics were oddly mixed—a raccoon with squirrel ears and tail, a bear with reptilian scales, a bird with fish fins, all of them weirdly cute. Carter was thankful there weren't any mechanical spiders running around with baby-doll heads, at least. He thought watching *Toy Story* with Thad for the first time years ago had scarred him permanently, though Thad had never seemed bothered by the neighbor kid's creepy creations.

"This is great, Erin."

She shrugged ahead of him as she started up the stairs. "The kids seem to like it."

"I can see why." It had him thinking...and wanting to ask. He shouldn't, he knew. The less he delved into her personal life, the better.

Oh, fuck it.

"You never had any children?" he probed carefully.

The straight line of Erin's shoulders ahead of him sank the slightest bit. "No." At the top of the stairs, she half turned toward him. "Stephen and I were both only children, so no nieces or nephews either. Just me." She shrugged again, but he sensed a downturn in her mood.

"You obviously have an aptitude with kids," he offered. "Thad can't stay away from you."

"It's my magnetic personality," she joked. Gesturing into one of the rooms off the hallway, she asked, "Wanna help me hang some lights?"

They chatted easily—surprising in and of itself—as they worked together. He'd expected more tension between them, but the only tension he felt rising was sexual. Having Erin so close to him, her body brushing against his, her fingers tangling with his as they worked to get the lights strung and cords hidden made things below his belt tighten in a way he was glad JD wasn't here to witness.

"Where is that last box?" Erin said absently, searching the corner of the room where various boxes and packaging had been piled. "I don't see it."

"Where is everything stored? I'll go get it."

Erin waved away his suggestion. "It will be in the attic. I'll go."

He decided to tag along anyway. He could even admit to himself that he wasn't ready to part from her company. He *wouldn't* admit that his gaze was glued to her backside the entire climb—though what a backside it was. Most of the time Erin was dressed in baggy coveralls that hid the details of her curves, but maybe because they'd been to the pub tonight before coming over to work, she was wearing snug jeans and a sweater that stopped at her waist, giving him an excellent view. He had to deliberately train his gaze on something else before they reached the attic or he'd surely give the game away if she granted him a single glance—his body wasn't keen on hiding anything at the moment. Thank goodness she went straight to searching the remaining boxes stacked around the floor. Carter crossed the room to stare out of the fan-shaped window that faced the front of the house, hoping to give himself a bit of breathing space.

"Wow." The view that greeted him was far lovelier than he'd anticipated. The window was wide enough that it allowed for a view encompassing the east side of downtown at one end and the mountains and valleys in the distance to the other. It was a panorama anyone could appreciate, especially with the last hints of sunlight peeking over the mountains to glint off the autumn colors of the trees at the farthest reach of his gaze.

Erin came up beside him and set down a cardboard box before putting all her attention on the view. "Right?" The sigh that crossed her lips was almost wistful. "The house belonged to the original mayor of Black Wolf's Bluff, so when it went vacant several years ago, the town bought it, but they haven't invested funds to fix it up yet." She glanced around. "We get to use it for the haunted house each year, but the idea of seeing it in all its former glory…"

That was definitely wistfulness in her tone. "Have you ever thought about doing it yourself?"

Her gaze swept the floor. "I can't afford a pet project like that. I'd need to live here, and I can't move away from Scott and Ruth."

"Why not?"

She shot him a startled glance, and he shrugged. "Scott seemed really nice from what I gathered"—on such a short meeting, five minutes tops once Erin and Thad had corralled the reluctant calf back into the barnyard with its mama—"but if it was what you really wanted, I would think they'd want to see you happy."

"Oh, they would. It's all they've really wanted for me. They treat me more like a daughter than a daughter-in-law."

"But that doesn't extend to you possibly moving down the road a bit?"

Her mouth twisted slightly. "They're getting older. Scott has already had one scare."

Right, the day Erin had almost run them off the road.

"I couldn't forgive myself if I wasn't there and something happened."

"You're not there every day, Erin," he reminded her, keeping his voice gentle. And oddly enough, it really wasn't that hard. Instead of the fierce contention that had lain between them since day one, he found himself instead wanting to help fulfill the longing underlining her words.

"I'm not. But having a field hand and not living there at all are two different things."

They were; he certainly understood that. Being able to contact Thad at all times, knowing he was safe with his mother, wasn't the same as living with him 24-7.

"Anyway, I've got a home already."

He bit down on the inside of his cheek, keeping the words on the tip of his tongue inside. He wasn't a part of Erin's life, no matter how well it was coming to feel like they knew each other. No matter how explosive their reactions were to one another. He had no business poking into her life, her dreams.

"We'd better get these lights hung." Erin turned abruptly, caught her toe on a floorboard, and stumbled into a stack of lumber next to her. An exasperated cry filled the air.

"What is it? You okay?"

Her back was to him, and he could see she was fiddling

with something in front of her. "It's fine," she said, impatience creeping in. "Just fine—oh!"

She stumbled backward, right into Carter's arms.

"Damn it!"

He situated her on her feet, then attempted to circle around. "Erin—"

"No, don't!" She held up a hand, the other going to the front of her shirt, right over her breasts. "It's fine."

He begged to differ but decided waiting her out was better than arguing. She mumbled to herself, fiddling with her sweater. Finally an irritated sigh left her.

"Now will you tell me what the problem is?"

She mumbled again, this time to him.

"What?"

"I tore my sweater."

"Okay."

She sighed impatiently. "I ripped it open. Over my…chest."

"Over…" Oh. His gut clenched, imagining what she was describing, what she still wouldn't let him see.

"Damn it." She turned around, a hand between her breasts. Not only must there be a tear beneath her fingers, but he could see the edges of the hole extending even farther, showing a bit of her belly and cleavage. "I can't go down there like this."

Neither could he, apparently—just the sight of that tiny bit of creamy skin had his dick pushing hard against his zipper. "You can just hold it until—"

"I don't have any extra clothes," she said. "I keep some in my truck, usually—you never know what's gonna happen on a job site. But my truck isn't here, remember?"

"Right." He licked his lips, trying to remember why he shouldn't stare at her chest. "Uh…"

"Carter!"

Her sharp tone snapped him out of his fascination. "Yeah?"

"I need a solution here."

He forced his mind toward the practical. "Got it." Reaching behind his head, he grasped the neck of his Henley and pulled it up and over. "Here."

Once the shirt was off his body, he handed it over, using his opposite hand to smooth the undershirt he'd worn against the chill autumn air down his belly.

Erin stared at the proffered shirt like it might bite. "What?"

"Wear my shirt. It'll cover you just fine." He could just imagine it draping across her breasts, the soft swell visible in his mind's eye. Yes, he definitely wanted her to wear his shirt.

"Oh. Um, okay."

Erin grasped the fabric, and his stomach quivered when her skin slid along his. As he waited, she took the shirt in hand, then turned her back to him. He wasn't certain what he'd expected, but it definitely wasn't for her to drop his shirt on top of the board she'd caught her sweater on, grasp the edges of her top, and whip it off over her head, leaving him face to back with her naked skin and a strap of pretty red lace crossing just beneath her shoulder blades.

His breath caught in his throat. "Erin?"

CHAPTER
Fourteen

A sharp gasp behind her froze Erin in place. Chill air raced across her bare arms, bare stomach, nearly bare breasts.

Bare.

What the hell had she done?

She stood there, frozen, the reality that she'd whipped her sweater off in front of the man who'd kissed her like he was starving for her—and she'd kissed him back just as hungrily—actually coming alive in her mind. She didn't even know why she'd done it. If it had been one of her girlfriends there, sure, she'd have tossed it off no problem, but Carter?

Oh God, she was naked in front of Carter.

"Erin?"

Her name was a wheeze on his lips, as if his lungs had frozen. In disgust? Shock? Horror that she was about to proposition him?

She wasn't. Was she?

"Erin," he said again, the word only slightly less strained, "is that red lace?"

This time it was Erin that gasped. Because that wasn't

disgust or horror in Carter's voice. No, it was something far more dangerous.

She glanced over her shoulder, barely taking him in from the corner of her eye. "Yes," she managed to squeeze out.

She might be most comfortable in chunky overalls and flannel shirts, but she had a secret, something very few people knew about her. A secret fascination with sexy lingerie. And what she had on right now, beneath her snug jeans and softest sweater, clothes she'd worn because they were going to the pub tonight—oh, who was she kidding? She'd worn them because she'd known she would see Carter tonight—was her sexiest lace bra and panty set. Red lace. Completely see-through.

A muttered curse came from behind her, and then she felt Carter's heat close in on her back. Felt the heavy sigh that escaped him as he stared down at her bare skin.

"Let me see."

If the words had been a demand, she could have easily said no. But there was no arrogance in Carter's request. He was begging—

And she couldn't deny him.

She turned around.

"Holy shit!"

Beneath her disbelieving eyes, Carter went to his knees in front of her. That alone was astonishing, but the fact that he reached for her, hands trembling, nearly undid her. The realization that this sophisticated man with his devilishly handsome face and stern outlook on life could be literally brought to his knees, *trembling,* at the sight of her bare body did things to her she wasn't certain she wanted to acknowledge. She did know her throat got tight and her breasts swelled, seeming to reach for him as his fingers hovered over the lace-covered orbs.

"You're beautiful," he breathed. The gust hit her skin, tightening her nipples, and he groaned before his hands cupped the outsides of each breast and he leaned forward to take one hardened tip into his mouth.

Erin startled. Moaned. Arched. Her fingers dug into those short blond strands at the back of his head, pulling him closer, begging silently for him to take more of her inside. And Carter complied. His mouth opened wider, his teeth surrounded her nipple, and he sucked hard, a sound of sheer hunger escaping as he took her deep. Thick masculine fingers dug into her soft mounds, her ribs, forcing her closer. A hard male chest pressed against her thighs. She'd forgotten what it felt like to have a mouth at her breast, to feel that ravenous hunger taking her in, to feel the sheer weight and strength of a male body against hers, and she reveled in it, in him. The only thing that would make it better would be to get closer to him, as close as humanly possible.

"God, Erin," he groaned as he released her.

She whined, her hands pulling him to her opposite breast without thought. She needed him to keep going. "Don't stop," she begged breathlessly.

"No stopping," he mumbled against her nipple, the brush of his lips dragging a moan from deep inside her, and then he had her in his mouth again. A zing of lightning shot down her stomach, hitting her clit like a mini bomb. The detonation brought her to her knees.

Seeming to sense what she needed, Carter didn't let go. His hand against her butt kept her upright, straddling one of his bent legs. She settled onto his thigh, his hand sliding up between her shoulder blades to steady her as he pressed her backward, his mouth moving in a frenzy against her breast. It felt so good—the wet suction on her nipple, the hungry pressure tugging and tugging, drawing her out of herself even as it sent waves of incredible pleasure straight through her body. The probing of thick fingers against the apex of her thighs had her tilting her hips, opening herself to him, giving him access until finally the pads of his fingertips settled on her most sensitive spot and dragged in a circle, nearly shooting her straight into the atmosphere.

Her hands shot to his shoulders, fingers digging in, hanging on for dear life. "Carter! Oh God, Carter, please."

His laugh was a little pleased and a whole lot desperate, a feeling she could relate to. She didn't let herself think, didn't wonder how in the world they'd gotten from mutually antagonistic to desperate for each other in the space of a few hours. All she knew was that she needed him, needed this, now. Right now.

His circling pressed the seam of her jeans against her clit. Erin could feel the rise of her orgasm, felt the tingles of impending ecstasy. Instinct had her shifting closer until her knee met Carter's crotch. The thick ridge of his cock was unmistakable, and just the thought of having him inside her shot shivers of desire into her center. "Not yet," she whimpered. Not yet. It was too good. She wanted it to last; she wanted to come. The war of needs fought deep inside her gut, echoing the pressure of Carter's manipulative fingertips against her clit. Soft, slow. Hard, fast. Over and over, the dizzying whirlwind went round and round, accompanied by the steady rocking of his cock against her knee.

She couldn't go on forever, no matter how much she might wish to. When Carter bit down on her nipple, his fingers sliding roughly along the top of her clit to press hard at the opening to her body, she detonated like a supernova, lighting up the night sky. She was vaguely aware of Carter grunting against her breast, of wet warmth against her knee, but she couldn't quite bring herself to interpret what she felt. All she could focus on was the spasms of her body and the soft, sweet feel of Carter's hair twisted in her fingers.

Long moments later, soothing strokes of big hands trailing up and down her spine registered. A tight, firm chest pressed to hers. Heavy breaths gusted against the strap of her bra over her bare shoulder.

Holy hell, he hadn't even gotten her bra off.

What would happen if he did?

The thought sent her scrambling to her feet, curses ripping the air. She'd had sex—or practically had sex...*almost* had sex?—with her best friend's fiancé's best friend. That was wrong, right? Or...right, wrong.

She growled. *Damn it!*

She was afraid to look at him, so she sneaked a peek out of the corner of her eye. The room had gotten gloomier the longer they'd been here, but it still wasn't dark enough that she couldn't see him there, still kneeling, a dark patch clearly evident at the crotch of his jeans. He wasn't looking at her; he was staring at his hands, fisted on his knees. Angry? Of course he was angry. Or, no...why would he be angry? He was the one who'd touched her. But she'd whipped her shirt off. So, yeah, angry. Right?

Would you stop asking yourself what's right? Get away from him and figure it out later!

Tough to do when he was literally her ride home.

"Carter—"

"I'm sorry."

He was sorry.

All the emotion roiling inside her deflated. Well, not all the emotion. Apparently she could be angry just fine. And she didn't care if it was *right*.

"Of course you are."

He lifted his head, blinking. "What?"

"Of course you're 'sorry.'" Yes, in her anger she even made air quotes.

"Well, now I'm confused."

She crossed her arms over her breasts and frowned at him.

"What's going on, Erin?"

She hated the fact that she loved how he said her name. "You tell me."

He shook his head. "I'm not playing games with you, not

anymore." Rising from his knees, he pushed his jean legs down, grimacing as the wet material dragged across his skin. "Tell me what's going on in that head of yours."

"That head of mine? What does that mean?"

He arched his brows. "That you have a head and it belongs to you?"

She didn't want to have this conversation right now; that's what was going on. She'd never acted like that in her life, not with someone she barely knew. She and Stephen had been young and impetuous, but they'd known each other for a lifetime before sex had entered the picture. In this town it was difficult to meet anyone she hadn't at least heard tales about. She'd certainly never expected someone she'd met mere days ago to set her off like a freaking rocket.

Lord.

"Erin." Carter started across the room.

"Wait." She put up a hand, one she knew was shaking but couldn't seem to stop it.

It didn't stop Carter either. He kept coming until that hand was enveloped in his and he was pulling her to him.

"I don't want—"

"I'm not coming on to you, damn it." The words were harsh, but his touch was gentle. "Just let me hold you for a minute."

Her head jerked up in surprise. She hadn't expected that from him. Guess there were a lot of things she hadn't expected from him—and she didn't know how she felt about any of it.

Carter pulled her in despite the stiffness of her body. It was his heat that undid her as much as the gesture. Warmth surrounded her now chilled skin, sinking inside her, stilling the confusion for the briefest moment, long enough for her to think beyond the panic. Long enough for her to melt against him, and once she had, she found pulling back was impossible.

"I don't understand this," she finally admitted, her head tucked against his shoulder.

His chuckle was shaky. "I don't either, but I'm not gonna get upset about it."

"I guess you do this often, huh?"

He jerked back enough to look down at her. "What is that supposed to mean?"

She sighed, shaking her head. "Nothing. It doesn't mean anything except I can't control whatever's popping out of my mouth right now."

His grin was lopsided, almost boyish with the hint of curls falling over his forehead and the tension he'd seemed to carry since he'd arrived dissolved from his face. "Erin Jenkins, speechless?"

She gave the spare flesh at his side a light pinch. "Not speechless. Just…not…" She sighed. "I have no idea."

He eased closer until his stubble was brushing her cheek and his lips were at her ear. "Me too."

They clung together there, in the darkening attic, the silence full of an emotion she refused to put a name to. And even when she'd pulled his shirt on, retrieved her ruined sweater, and headed down the stairs, she kept her mouth closed, unsure of what, if anything, to say.

CHAPTER
Fifteen

E rin's gaze met Carter's as she exited the SUV, but it was too dark to see his expression clearly. JD's presence kept her from speaking. Regret shimmered inside as she climbed the steps to her porch—not regret for what they'd done, but regret that they hadn't discussed it, hadn't spoken since they'd descended from the attic and found JD searching for them on the first floor. Luckily a quick explanation remedied the issue of Carter's shirt on Erin's body and her ruined sweater in his grip had covered the wet spot at his crotch. The night had proceeded from there, but that didn't change the fact that she and Carter had badly needed to talk and hadn't.

Willard had roosted for the night, allowing Erin to cross the porch unaccosted. Weariness dragged at her limbs. Though she'd always been one of those people that dropped into sleep the minute her head hit the pillow, a fact Stephen had often teased her about, tonight she found herself staring at the ceiling, unable to drift off.

Unable to stop thinking about Carter.

Images flitted across her mind's eye—the husky note in

his voice when he'd asked her to turn around, the gleam of hunger in his eyes as he'd approached her, the strength in the fingers that had stroked her body. It had all been unexpected and yet so, so good. Why? Two days ago she could have sworn he couldn't stand her.

But that kiss had changed everything. And tonight?

Lord a'mercy, tonight hadn't just changed everything; it felt like it had changed *her*.

It wasn't even so much the pleasure of the act that had her mind blown. Oh, the pleasure had shocked her, no doubt about it, but she'd acknowledged days ago that the two of them had a chemistry that both intrigued and alarmed her. She just hadn't expected it to be so explosive.

Still, it wasn't just the pleasure. It was how she saw herself. For so long it had been Erin the contractor, Erin the friend. Erin the daughter-in-law. Not Erin the lover, or mate, or even woman. But there was no denying that those moments with Carter in the attic had been all about Erin the woman. It was an awakening she hadn't expected, and now, she wasn't sure if she wanted to continue being awake or go back to sleep.

Actually, no, she didn't want to go back to sleep. She simply had no idea what moving forward entailed.

Four thirty found her in her sleepshirt on the front porch swing, the breeze cooling her body through the thin weave of the afghan she'd wrapped around herself, the dark and quiet soothing the riot of emotions roiling inside her. The few restless hours of sleep she'd managed had been interrupted by a hot and heavy dream of Carter, of the two of them going a lot farther than they had up in that attic—and because they'd been desperately close already, the details her mind supplied had seemed disturbingly real. Unable to return to sleep, she'd wandered out here. Sunrise arrived later this time of the year, so it was still dark when lights came on in Ruth and Scott's house shortly after five. The farmhand she'd hired, Bryan, drove up at the same time. He was young, still attending the community college up in Morristown, but a contractor friend of hers had recommended him and so far he'd been perfect. He was able to come early mornings and most evenings, and Scott certainly hadn't been lifting bales of hay since Bryan had started a couple of days ago.

She watched from her porch as the two men walked toward the barn. Ruth followed behind and emerged a few minutes later with a basket of eggs over her arm. She walked toward Erin's house, using the gate in the fence to enter the yard and beeline toward the front porch. When she noticed Erin on the swing, a sweet smile took over her wrinkled face.

"What are you doing out here so early in the morning? Trouble sleeping?"

Erin bent her knees and pulled her legs closer, giving Ruth room to sit at the opposite end of the swing. "Yeah."

Ruth set the basket on the porch and took a seat. Her still-strong hand felt thin on Erin's leg. "Nightmares?"

When Stephen had first been gone, she'd had nightmares frequently. "No, not nightmares." Thank goodness those had faded over the years, superseded by happier memories of her husband. She couldn't bring herself to tell Ruth she'd been dreaming about another man, though.

When the silence stretched on, Ruth squeezed her ankle. "Gonna tell me about it?"

Tell her mother-in-law about dry humping her best friend's guest? No. "Just some things on my mind."

"Like what, Bug?" When Erin just smiled, Ruth hummed thoughtfully. "It wouldn't have anything to do with that nice young man you've been seeing, now would it?"

Erin startled. "Carter?" How had she guessed?

Ruth's eyebrows hit her hairline. "I was thinking about the little boy—Thad, right?" She gave Erin a look. "But let's talk about Carter instead."

Shit. Erin covered her face with a hand, a groan escaping. "How about let's not?"

Ruth snickered. "Too late."

A sigh escaped that felt like it started in Erin's toes.

"That bad, huh?"

Or that good, depending on what they were talking about. "I just don't get it."

Ruth turned toward Erin and drew her knee up onto the swing, her arm across the back. Getting comfortable. "Get what?"

"Him? Me? Any of it?" Erin propped her elbow on the back of the swing as well and dug her fingers into her hair to cradle her head. "I mean, Stephen and I got along so well; it was like we were one person. We met when we were so young. Everything felt...seamless. We never argued, fought. We teased, sure, but..."

"I take it the same can't be said for Carter."

Erin's growl said it all if Ruth's grin was anything to go by.

"Okay, that is good to know." Ruth patted Erin's ankle. "Yes, you and Stephen's relationship was seamless, but it was also very different circumstances, and you know what they say, Bug—variety is the spice of life."

Erin rubbed the side of her head in frustration. "Carter definitely adds spice."

"Sounds like it. And that's not necessarily a bad thing."

"I think it is."

Ruth's laugh was deep and full. "Got your knickers in a twist, does he?"

"In more ways than one."

When Erin realized what she'd said, she slapped a hand over her mouth, but Ruth just laughed again. Waving away Erin's comment—thank God—she asked, "Have I ever told you how Scott and I met?"

Erin shook off her embarrassment. "Of course you have."

That would have been in the late '60s, here in rural Tennessee where the teen social scene had been more like the '50s. "At an ice cream social, right?"

"Mmm." Ruth's eyes went unfocused, her attention obviously drawn back to memories of that time. "Did I tell you I dumped my ice cream soda over his head within ten minutes of meeting him?"

"What?" Erin shrieked. She crossed her legs, leaning over them to get closer to Ruth. "Why? And why did you never tell me about that?"

"Well, you know…" Ruth's smile was soft. "I didn't want you to think badly of Scott, though truth be told, it was as much my fault as his. We met, and sparks flew, only they weren't all good sparks, not at first." She chuckled. "There was plenty of…oh, what do you young folks call it now? Chemistry? Whatever it was, we both fought it from the get-go."

"I can't imagine the two of you fighting." In all the years she'd known them, Scott and Ruth had seemed the perfect couple, happy, affectionate. Her marriage to Stephen had been similar, but Ruth was right—they'd grown up together, known each other so long, that it was really no surprise they'd gotten along so well.

Ruth and Scott had certainly never seemed the least bit volatile. Not like her and Carter.

"Like cats and dogs at first," Ruth assured her. "But that stopped soon enough."

"Why?"

"He kissed me."

Erin's cheeks went pink. Ruth took in the color, giving her a knowing look in the rising light of dawn as it peaked over the ridge. "So you know too." She nodded sagely. "Sometimes we just don't know what to do with all that attraction, but eventually we figure it out."

"What?" When Ruth's meaning registered, Erin sputtered,

her face going even hotter despite the chill autumn air. "I don't… Um… We didn't…"

"You may not have had sex—"

Oh God.

"But you definitely know what I'm talking about," Ruth countered, obviously amused. "Good."

"Good?"

"Of course. You weren't meant to live as a nun."

Laughter escaped despite Erin's complete mortification at this entire conversation.

They sat like that for a few minutes, Erin embarrassed, Ruth thoughtful. It was Ruth who finally broke the silence.

"You know Stephen wouldn't want you to live by yourself forever."

No, he wouldn't have, and she did know it. But… "I'm not looking for anybody new." She hadn't been before Carter entered the scene, and she certainly hadn't been afterward.

Now…

"Sometimes when you're not looking is when life surprises you. There's so much more out there for you than watching over two old people and a farm while you work at a career that you love but can't love you back."

And wasn't that what Erin had been thinking earlier? She saw herself as Erin the contractor, not Erin the woman. But she was a woman, and something about Carter's touch had awakened that part of her with unexpected ferocity.

Ruth gave her another pat. "I better go let Willard out." She stirred and bent to pick up her basket. "Why don't you take some of these before I use the rest to make the men breakfast."

Erin stood. "How about I make you breakfast? Give me a few minutes to get dressed."

"I'll be waiting," Ruth called back cheerfully as she descended the steps. Erin hurried inside, knowing Ruth would start cooking with or without her. But even as she got ready for the day, her thoughts continued to circle.

CHAPTER
Sixteen

Two deep voices drifted from the kitchen as Carter approached far too early Friday morning. Thoughts of Erin—the feel of her lace-covered nipples in his mouth, the sheer pleasure filling her face as she'd gone over the edge—had kept him awake late into the night. Those thoughts had likely been the cause of the explicit dream that had forced him into the shower to jack off before dawn. What he really wanted was to return to bed, but Thad was still sleeping and Carter didn't want to risk waking him, so coffee would have to do.

The voices went quiet as Carter entered the kitchen. Then, "Hey, bro!"

Carter stopped in his tracks. "Linc? Hey! What are you doing here?"

Linc charged across the kitchen to give Carter a bear hug. "I'm surprising Claire. Get to stay till Sunday, same as you."

Carter returned the hug before crossing the room to the coffee maker. "Thought you were out in Cali for one of those press things."

"Junket," JD said around a mouthful of omelet.

"Whatever." His brain was still half-asleep, so coughing up words wasn't a priority.

"That's why it's such a quick trip," Linc explained. "Claire has talked about the harvest festival so much I knew it would mean a lot if I could manage to get here."

"Mm." Carter turned from the now half-empty coffeepot with his full cup, raising it toward his mouth, when he spotted JD's plate and did a double take. "Hey, do I get one of those?"

Linc rolled his eyes and grumbled his way over to the stove, something about only being appreciated for what you did for people.

Carter chuckled. "Don't be an idiot. It's not you we appreciate; it's the food."

Linc raised a middle finger at him with one hand and turned on the stove with the other.

A hum of delight was Carter's response—to the smooth heat of the coffee as he took his first sip, not Linc's gesture. That he ignored, walking right by to settle himself at the table with JD.

"Thad still sleeping?" JD asked.

"Yeah." When his cup was safely on the tabletop, Carter pulled out his phone. No messages. Disappointment thumped in his chest. He and Erin had left a lot unspoken last night. He'd hoped she'd text him after they'd dropped her off, but there'd been nothing when he got home and nothing now.

> Carter: Need a ride this morning?

He waited a moment, but no little bubbles appeared to show a text coming in.

> Carter: Thad is still snoozing. Thought we might get a chance to talk.

"Hey, do you want bell peppers?"

Carter wrinkled his nose across the kitchen at Linc. "Hell no."

"Just mushrooms. Come on, Linc, you know that," JD said.

"I can't remember y'all's picky shit."

Carter raised eyebrow. "'Y'all'?"

JD leaned close as if sharing a secret. "Too much time with Claire."

"Ah"—Linc raised his spatula in the air—"there's no such thing."

"So says the fancy New York City chef whose vocabulary now includes 'y'all.'" Carter smirked.

"It also includes 'kick your ass.'"

JD shook his head. "Don't mind him, Carter. He's just testy from a long flight."

"No, he's pretty much always like this."

Linc lifted one edge of the omelet to peek at the underside. "Do you want me to spit in your eggs?"

JD pulled a face. "I'd definitely go with testy, Carter."

Linc grinned. "Hey, you know how I feel about food; I'm actually more likely to spit on him than the omelet."

Carter choked on his sip of coffee.

JD made a gagging noise. "Gross." He slapped Carter on the back a couple of times. Carter was pretty sure the assistance made his coughing worse, not better. "Anyway, Carter has his own woman troubles. He should be paying attention to those instead of how your woman has influenced your vocabulary."

Omelet plated, Linc headed for the table, brows raised. "Woman troubles? Tell me all about it, bro."

"How about let's not," Carter muttered, accepting his plate.

But JD barged right in. "He and Erin haven't exactly hit it off this visit."

"He and Erin?" Linc repeated the words as if they were incomprehensible. "Sweet little Erin?"

"Sweet?" Carter scoffed. Erin was a lot of things—good things—but sweet wasn't one he'd put at the top of the list. Of course, it appeared that was what he liked about her.

Go figure.

Linc narrowed his eyes on Carter. "Of course Erin is sweet. So what did you do to her?"

A smug smile crept across JD's face. "How did he guess that, huh?"

"Because I know him well?" Linc offered.

Carter chewed a piece of omelet—which was perfect, damn it—and frowned at them both.

"Okay, okay." JD held up his hands. "It was just a little misunderstanding."

Linc grunted against his coffee cup. "If I recall correctly, someone at this table told me in no uncertain terms not to mess with Lily's friends. Was that you?" he asked JD. "Did you give this guy"—he jerked his head toward Carter—"the same speech you gave me?"

"No, because he hadn't ruined Erin's career."

"That was a long time ago," Linc mumbled.

"For *y'all's* information," Carter said, forking up another bite, "Erin and I get along just fine now."

"Yeah. She was even wearing his shirt last night."

Carter squeezed his eyes shut. JD was supposed to forget that little tidbit. He glared his friend's way.

"Well, she was," JD said.

Linc frowned. "Whatever is going on, spill it."

"It's nothing."

"Of course it was nothing," JD said, though something about his tone now seemed uncertain.

"Not buying it," Linc added.

From the corner of Carter's eye, he saw JD lower his cup

slowly to the table, his light blue eyes narrowing. When an incredulous look replaced it, Carter knew his time was up.

"Carter? What exactly have you been doing with Erin?" JD asked.

"I'm not doing anything with Erin." Not anything he wanted to tell these two about.

JD sighed. "You might as well spill, bro. You know we'll find out eventually."

On the table, Carter's cell phone vibrated. A quick glance told him it was a text from Erin. Anticipation sent his belly into a flip.

> Erin: I could use a ride. Pick me up at the farm?

Not exactly forthcoming, but she hadn't said no. Carter pushed back his chair, abandoning his food and coffee. "JD, can you keep an eye out for Thad? I'll be back soon."

"Where are you going?"

"Out."

He snagged his running shoes and keys in the foyer and was through the door before anyone could get out another question.

On the ride through town, Carter enjoyed the sunrise even as the question of Erin continued to nag at him. Granted, he'd dated often enough since his divorce. Maybe it had been an expectation from the people around him, or maybe he'd just wanted to appear "normal," whatever that meant. A part of him hadn't wanted anyone to realize how strongly the breakup of his marriage had shaken him. He needed to be strong for Thad, right? Needed to hide the fractured parts of himself and give them time to heal unquestioned. He'd even gone along with Emma's little games despite wishing most of the time that he could simply stay home with a good book.

And yet none of the encounters he'd had on those dates

had generated the kind of emotions Erin did from day one. Sure, the first emotion had been anger, but looking back he could see how that anger had been closely intertwined with a desire not to give in to the chemistry that had immediately flared between them at that very first meeting.

When he drove into the valley, he took the first driveway this time, pulling in behind a couple of pickups and a station wagon that, despite its age, seemed well-maintained. Erin wasn't waiting on the porch, so he turned off the SUV and headed for the door. He wasn't certain if that's what she wanted or not, but he knew he didn't want to hide their relationship—or whatever this was—even from her family. That much he was clear about. No, last night hadn't been expected, but it had happened and he didn't regret it. Nor was he ashamed. He wanted to get to know Erin more, and this was his opportunity to prove it.

As he stepped onto the porch, the front door opened and Erin's mother-in-law, Ruth, gave him a sweet smile. "Come in, come in. We're just finishing up breakfast. Have you eaten?"

"I definitely wouldn't turn down food." He opened the old-fashioned screen door and was surprised to find himself enveloped in a bear hug the minute he stepped inside.

"It's so good to see you again."

Her tone was genuine, warming his heart. "Thank you, Ruth. It's good to see you too." He meant it. These people were a huge part of Erin's life, and he could finally admit he wanted to find out what that life was like.

The welcome wasn't quite as warm in the kitchen, with Scott giving him a bit of a glower as he entered. Erin glanced up and quickly shoveled another bite into her mouth. "Almost done," she mumbled.

Carter was too busy taking in the braids angling down each side of her bare neck to reply. He felt like he shouldn't, but he was becoming fascinated with those braids.

Ruth made up for his silence. "Don't you rush, Bug. I'm just going to get Carter a plate."

Eyebrows all around the table rose as he took a seat. He gave Erin a questioning glance, but her surprise quickly morphed into something that looked like pleasure. "I'll take a little more time then." Giving him a wink, she held up a flaky biscuit. "These aren't to be missed, by the way."

He grinned. "Good to know."

"Coffee, Carter?" Ruth asked.

"I can get that," Carter said.

"Stay where you are," Erin told him. Getting up from the table, she rounded behind him and slid her hand along his shoulder blades as she passed. "I'll grab it and get some more while I'm up."

She returned to the table just ahead of Ruth, who'd loaded a plate down with hash browns and eggs and thick, crispy bacon. Two biscuits waited alongside.

Erin made a funny noise. "I didn't think. Can you have biscuits and potatoes? Carbs are like sugar, right?"

He appreciated the fact that she'd remembered. "I do have to watch the carbs, but I can have a little as long as I'm careful."

Ruth must have given her a questioning look, because Erin explained, "Carter is diabetic."

He held up his coffee cup. "Helps that I like black coffee," he joked.

"Oh, I can change that plate out for you," Ruth offered.

He waved her away. "No need. Sit down and eat. I might not clear my plate, but I definitely want a bite of what looks like a very good biscuit."

Ruth's cheeks went pink. "Well, okay."

Conversation returned to the general table after that, allowing Carter to listen instead of being the center of attention. Much to his delight, the biscuits were great—in fact, one of the best he'd ever tasted. The rest of the food as well.

Carter would never mention it to Linc, but the eggs rivaled even the famous chef's fluffy omelets.

He absorbed the give-and-take around the table as everyone finished up. The conversation was practical—a routine visit from the vet, moving hay into the barn for the winter, getting a new battery for Erin's truck, things like that —but the undertone of affection was noticeable. He found himself watching Erin, the play of the sunlight on her face, the affectionate way she called Scott and Ruth *Mom* and *Dad*, the laughter when one of her in-laws teased her. He thought he could have watched her all day, but finally the meal ended and, after assisting with clearing the table, they gave the group their goodbyes and headed out the door.

"Thanks for that, Erin."

She threw a smile over her shoulder. "I'm glad you enjoyed it. We don't get together every morning, but break-fast with the family is something I've always loved."

He felt the same way about meals with his own family.

As the SUV loomed large in front of them, Carter found himself getting nervous. Almost fifty years old and he was nervous about a conversation with a woman.

No, not just any woman. With Erin. The question was, could he get through one conversation without putting his foot in his mouth?

And if he did, what would be the outcome?

CHAPTER
Seventeen

C arter handed her into the SUV like an old-fashioned gentleman. A giggle bubbled up in her throat, but Erin squashed it ruthlessly. Nerves, it was just nerves. She wasn't a young girl giggling over some guy just because of a gallant gesture.

She might drool over him, but that was a different story.

To be honest, the change in their relationship was giving her whiplash. Even the word *relationship* was weird. This wasn't a relationship. More like a one-night stand, maybe, although she admitted to herself that she would like more. Carter gave her butterflies in her stomach—even back when he'd been acting like a jerk—but she also admired the way he parented Thad, the friendship he had with JD. He wasn't just the grumpy single dad she'd met a few days ago.

He also wasn't going to be around long. So where did that leave things?

Carter settled himself in the driver's seat and started the SUV. "Willard's not on the attack today, huh?"

She laughed even as the scent of cedar and man filled the space and sent tingles to places she probably shouldn't be thinking about with Carter in such close proximity. "Too busy gobbling up his own breakfast," she said absently. Sunlight glinted off Carter's strong hands on the steering wheel, the dusting of pale hairs on his forearms. She found herself fascinated, squirming at the memory of those hands on her body.

Carter chuckled, and for a moment she feared he'd noticed her attention, but instead of backing out of the drive, he sat for a minute staring out the windshield. When he finally turned to her, it was with amusement in his clear blue eyes. "I don't think I've been this nervous with a girl in the car since I was seventeen and hoping for a make-out session with Jenny Mitchell on the way home from junior prom."

For a moment all Erin could do was gape—the idea that she made Carter nervous was incomprehensible. But then she laughed too. "I guess you're never too old for awkward conversations, huh?" She glanced down at her hands twisting in her lap. "You're not the only one who's nervous."

He seemed as surprised as she had been. Those eyes searched her face, taking in every ounce of emotion she feared was transparent to his gaze. One strong hand left the steering wheel and reached over to grasp hers. "I guess there's nothing to be nervous about then, huh?"

Oh, there definitely was. "Maybe not."

Silence cocooned them for a few minutes, Carter concentrating on the drive, his hand enveloping hers, his thumb stroking the soft skin between her thumb and forefinger. Erin waited, unsure what she wanted to say.

"Erin, I…"

Her gut tightened.

Carter cleared his throat. "Last night was…unexpected."

That didn't tell her anything. Of course it had been unexpected.

"Good unexpected," he finally continued, "but unexpected."

Her breath left her in a rush. Carter squeezed her hand.

"You didn't think I arranged this little talk to brush you off, did you?"

She turned, bringing her knee up to allow herself to angle toward Carter, to see his face and read him a little better. "I honestly wasn't certain what you were going to say. I mean, we didn't start off on the best foot."

"To say the least."

"Right."

"And I know that was my fault."

Surprise jolted her. He flashed her that boyish grin again.

"Took you long enough to admit that," she teased.

"Yeah, well"—he scratched at the stubble on his jaw—"no one has ever said I'm not hardheaded. You can ask my sister; she'll tell you all about it."

Erin tucked that bit of knowledge away.

"I'm just saying, I know we didn't get off on the right foot, but…I do like you, Erin. I admire your work. I like seeing you with your family." He paused. "I like seeing you with my son."

She would have guessed that last part was hard to admit, but Carter breathed the words as if they were completely natural. All she heard was simple truth.

"Thank you." Something loosened inside her, a lock opening on the door to a place that hadn't been open in a long, long time. She took a deep breath. "Last night threw me for a loop, too."

"Good or bad?"

Her voice was barely a whisper. "Good."

Carter's whole body seemed to relax into the seat. He squeezed her hand hard. "I'm glad."

"Me too."

To an outsider it might have seemed like the most inane conversation to ever follow a hasty, hot, totally unexpected—and satisfying—sexual encounter. To Erin, it was a reassurance she'd known she needed but hadn't expected to get.

"So what next?" she asked quietly.

Several minutes passed before Carter responded. "So… you probably won't believe this, but right before I came down here, I swore off dating."

Her stomach sank.

"I realized that I hadn't really been dating because I wanted to, but because people expected me to. But now—" The look Carter gave her… There went those butterflies again. "Now I'm wondering if that was such a good decision." He came to a stop at the red light just outside the town square and turned in his seat to look at her. "I'd like to find out what's between us, Erin. I don't know how that works with me leaving Sunday and you living here, but I'm open to exploring it." He raised an eyebrow at her. "How about you?"

She held her breath, staring into his eyes. The openness there had her leaning forward, bringing her lips to his. They hadn't kissed last night, and she needed that now, needed to know if they fit together as intimately in this moment as they had hours before.

And oh, it was good. His lips were firm, mobile, giving as well as taking. He didn't hesitate—his tongue sneaked into her mouth and mated with hers. Heat traveled through her body to settle between her legs.

A honking horn broke them apart. Carter glanced into the rearview mirror and let off the brake. Erin gave a nervous laugh.

Carter broke the silence. "Well?"

"Well…" Cheeky ass. "I can't believe I'm saying this considering what a massive wrong foot we got off to, but I'd like to explore this too."

Carter shook his head. "You're never gonna let me live that down, are you?"

She grinned. "Oh, absolutely not."

As they continued through town, that quick kiss was all Erin could think about, that and the feel of Carter's hand surrounding hers, his fingers stroking her, his scent surrounding her. She knew she needed to calm down, get this runaway freight train under control, but the closer they got to the mansion, the faster her heart beat. JD's place didn't exactly offer privacy, but she couldn't help hoping for a few moments to explore things between them just a little further.

Maybe she *was* that giggling teen girl, being dropped off for a date she didn't want to end.

And maybe Carter was that teen boy, because when they reached JD's house, he didn't pull into the gate. He kept going, only slowing down when he neared the shed. The quiet that enveloped them when the SUV shut off allowed her to hear the fast rhythm of Carter's breathing, as fast as hers. Which meant—

A quick glance toward Carter's lap said her supposition was right. That was all she had time to think before Carter's seat belt was off, hers was released, and he hauled her toward him.

Their lips met over the console. Carter gripped her jaw, tilting her head to allow him access, and she opened her mouth, inviting him in. His taste was hot, hungry, his tongue urgent, his body pressing closer despite the obstacles between them. Their lips mated again and again as she reached out a hand, palm flat, to find his chest. The muscles beneath his shirt barely yielded to her touch. She desperately wanted the chance to explore, but not here, not in the car where anyone could drive by and see them.

She broke away. "Wanna come inside?"

A blush lit up her cheeks, but Carter didn't laugh. His gaze leveled on her with a desire that made her shiver. "I definitely would."

And if he did, it would definitely lead to more than what they'd done last night, if that look told her anything. Was that what she wanted?

God, yes.

The two of them were out of the car and entering the murky shed in a fast minute. A glance around had Erin hesitating. "Um…"

Carter's laugh was strained. "Am I too old to have sex on top of a table created from plywood and sawhorses?"

The fact that he mentioned sex—like, full-on sex—had her perking up. "I don't know about you being too old, or me for that matter, but I think that table is too…something…for us to have sex on top of it."

"Right." He moved ahead of her into the center of the small room before turning back to face her. "Then let's see how we can improvise." He winked. "Unbutton your shirt."

Holy crap, they were doing this. Really doing this. In her work shed. Now.

Okay.

Her fingers shook as she brought them to the buttons of her green-plaid flannel shirt. Carter eyed her like he wanted to consume her, stalking forward as he watched the gap in the fabric open little by little by little. Finally the flannel shirt came off, leaving behind a white tank underneath, the black lace of her bra showing clearly beneath the stretched fabric. She grasped the hem and pulled. The tee slid up her stomach, revealing creamy skin, over her breasts, and as Carter moved closer, she abandoned it to undo the front clasp of her bra. Cool air brushed bare skin. Her nipples tightened instinctively, whether from the temperature or Carter's hungry gaze on them, she wasn't sure.

"Erin."

The hoarse note in his voice sent shivers down her spine. "Yes?"

"The pants."

Feeling the need to balance the power playing out between them, she toyed with the button of her cargo pants. "What about the pants?"

Carter stopped inches away. "Undo them. Give me access."

Her fingers fumbled as she undid the button, slid down the zipper. Carter's gaze followed her movements even as his fingers were busy pulling off his sweatshirt, loosening the drawstring of his jogging pants, pushing the fabric lower on his hips until she could see the dark hair at his groin. His erection was firm, standing straight out as if it was a divining rod pointing directly at her. Leaving her zipper open, she eased the fabric over his cock and bared him to the cold air just as she was bare. Carter shivered, but that could've been a reaction to her fingers tracing the underside of his cock—the smooth skin, the thick vein, the ridge below the mushroom head that stood out in his excitement.

"I want you, Carter."

He kissed her then, his mouth hungry, his hand covering hers to tighten around him. She felt him thump in her grip, felt her heartbeat zoom out of control as his chest began heaving against hers.

He broke away. "I don't think this is going to take long, Erin," he growled. The chuckle that followed was strained, deep.

She licked her lips. "Me either."

Carter dropped his gaze, raised his hands to cup her breasts. She gasped, his touch sending an electric shock from her breasts to her core. The focus of her world narrowed to his hands, his fingers, and she didn't realize he was guiding her backward until the table nudged her backside.

Carter pinched lightly at her nipples. "Turn around."

Her head fell back, her fingers digging into his T-shirt-covered biceps and refusing to let go. "Can't," she groaned. "Don't want to."

His mouth on her nipple convinced her she'd made the right decision. The suction weakened her knees, but Carter kept her upright, close, unable to escape the sweet sensation of his lips on her breast. His cock against her stomach. Instead he forced her to endure the delicious torture until she was squirming constantly, desperate for more.

"Carter!"

As he released her, his teeth slid along her skin. Erin grunted out her pleasure.

He chuckled. "I'd really like to take all night with you, and one day soon I will, but I don't think we have that long right now. I'm not risking an interruption just to draw it out."

She gave him a smile. "In that case…"

He nipped her neglected nipple gently, then turned her in his arms to face the table. A firm hand between her shoulder blades bent her over. Planting her elbows on the plywood, she wiggled her hips against the shaft branding her with his heat. "About those pants—"

"I gotcha; don't worry." Her pants eased down, panties going with them. When they were safely midthigh, Carter cupped her ass just as he had her breasts.

"Christ."

Less admiring, more action.

"Carter—"

As if he heard the desperation in her voice, he moved closer. His warmth soaked into her chilled skin, but it was the heat of his cock as he angled it down between her legs that had her breath speeding up.

Carter hissed.

"What is it?"

His fingers dug into her hips before easing up. "I don't have any condoms. I left my wallet at the house."

Damn it. She tried to force away the heat clouding her mind, force herself to think clearly, carefully. "It's okay."

"What?"

"It's okay. I'm on birth control." Her periods had started going haywire about a year ago. Rather than spend more time bleeding than not, her gynecologist had suggested the pill.

Since she hadn't needed birth control with Stephen gone, the doctor had figured she had a couple of safe years before they'd need to explore alternatives.

"Erin, are you sure? That's a big step."

"I'm clean," she said over her shoulder. "But it's up to you."

He bent over her back, his forehead coming to rest on her shoulder. Strong arms circled under her, holding her close. "I'm clean too, but I want you to be absolutely certain."

"I'm certain," she told him. "I want you."

He nodded against her, and then, with a sigh of acceptance, he raised up, his hands moving to torture her nipples once more while he lined himself up with her exposed core. The sound that left him this time was more a moan of ecstasy.

Widening her stance, Erin let him in, desperate for him to hurry. Her arousal rose, driving toward the peak with no more than his fingers on her sensitive tips, but she wanted more, and finally she got it when Carter carefully pushed his way inside. She knew wet warmth greeted him because the glide was easy, smooth, pain-free. He stretched her wide, bottoming out deep inside her where she felt the kick of his cock as she squeezed down on his intrusion.

Carter groaned. Erin panted.

"Please," she begged.

Apparently he didn't want to wait either, because he eased back and thrust inside, then retreated, all the way out until only that wide head remained, then all the way back in until she thought she wouldn't be able to breathe, he filled her so full. Again. Then again. The rhythm picked up, and with no more than a quick tingle of warning, Erin felt her climax explode, taking her breath, taking her voice. Wiping everything outside this moment completely away.

A whine escaped as Carter continued thrusting through her spasms, seeking his own satisfaction. When one hand lowered and a calloused finger circled her clit, she went up on her toes, only to be held down by Carter's weight, his body. All she could do was accept the pleasure as it started all over again. The thrusts came faster, the circling sped up, and before she knew it, she was there, right at the peak, holding her breath as she hung at the precipice before Carter pushed harder than ever inside her, deep, deep, and the jerking of his release set hers off once more.

CHAPTER
Eighteen

C arter's mind was completely blown. He'd had plenty of sex—fast sex, slow sex, so-so sex. This was, by any definition of the word, a quickie.

And yet it had been some of the best sex of his life.

Erin felt so right in his arms, like she fit him perfectly. As they both caught their breath, he held her hard against him. She lay flat out on the plywood, T-shirt rucked up above her breasts, head turned to the side to rest her cheek on the table, eyes closed, belly and breastbone moving rapidly beneath his hands to fill her lungs after the exertion. No attempt to get up, get away, get her clothes straightened out. She simply rested there, letting him put his weight on her, letting him enjoy the feel of her warmth around his softening cock. Her wet warmth.

Maybe it had been stupid to trust her, but he had. He'd looked into her eyes and seen truth there. Getting inside her, bare, feeling her arousal coating him with slick heat… God, there'd been nothing like it. And he definitely wanted it again. Wanted her again.

Before the thought could have him hardening inside her, he straightened, slid back, regret slamming him as his cock fell away from her body. Not for what they'd done, but for having to leave her.

He pulled Erin up from the table, cuddled her back against his front. Covered her breasts with his hands, offering her his heat. "Wow."

Erin chuckled against him. "I'd say."

"I want a lot more than a few minutes, Erin," he whispered in her ear.

She tilted her head, allowing him to nuzzle the soft skin of her neck. "I do too."

Pulling her hard against him, he dared to ask, "Tonight?"

When she pulled away, his heart tripped in his chest, but she only turned to face him, to bring her mouth up to his for a kiss. "Okay."

The sound of branches cracking outside had them both scrambling to straighten their clothes before whoever was out there interrupted, although Carter was pretty sure he knew exactly who it was. When Thad poked his head through the shed door, he found them both appropriately dressed. "Dad! Erin!"

"Hey, buddy."

"Hey!" He moved inside, his busy hands touching everything he came into reaching distance of. Except the saws; Carter noticed he stayed well away, per Erin's explicit instructions. "Uncle JD said you went to get Erin 'cause her truck isn't fixed. When will it be fixed, Erin? Did you know Uncle Linc is here? He came for the festival and we're making a fire tomorrow night in the fire pit to roast marshmallows and have s'mores. And Miss Claire is bringing special sugar-free marshmallows. Will you come? You could come to the festival with us tonight? Can you do that? Do you like s'mores?"

Carter laughed as he grabbed his son around the shoulders and hauled him in for a hug. "Take a breath, son. Erin can't answer you if you don't give her a chance to get a word in."

Thad grinned up at him, that slightly crooked smile that reminded Carter of his own smile in school pictures at that age. "Sorry." He peeked up at Erin from beneath his blond curls. "So will you go?"

Erin reached out to ruffle Thad's head. "I'll go." She took a deep breath. "But right now it is still a workday and I do have to actually work, so let me get to it, okay? The sooner I start, the sooner I can finish."

"Okay!" Thad threw his arms around Erin's waist. A fist squeezed down on Carter's heart.

"Okay," Erin repeated, returning Thad's hug.

When his son let her go, Carter moved in, giving her a kiss on one smooth cheek. "We'll see you later."

Erin met his gaze, her own sparkling with a mixture of what looked like amusement and anticipation. "Looking forward to it."

He ushered Thad out, daring one last look back at Erin before he slipped through the shed door. She looked disheveled, her hair coming out of her braids, her flannel shirt thrown on but not buttoned, her cargo pants straight and zipped but not nearly as attractive fully on as they'd looked around her thighs while he was driving hard inside her. And yet the sight of her made his dick twitch in a way that had him giving her a wink before he hastened out the door.

As usual, Thad talked all the way back to the mansion. After JD and Linc threw him knowing glances, Carter hastened into a quick shower before setting out on today's promised trip with JD and Lily to visit her grandfather. Henry Easton was in his late eighties, a tall, lanky man who still called Lily *punkin* and had the energy of someone half his age. He kept up with Thad easily as the group wandered all over Easton Cove, the former park ranger teaching them about the plants and animals of the Smoky Mountains. They caught sight of a fox scrambling over the boulders in the creek behind Henry's house, several salamanders and fish. A pair of cardinals and even an owl cleverly camouflaged against the bark of a tree. At one point they climbed to the ridge overlooking the next valley, and Henry pulled out some binoculars to show Thad a big black bear wandering through a far thicket. Carter's heart nearly thumped out of his chest at the sight of the dangerous animal, but Henry assured them they were a safe distance away. Still, Carter didn't breathe fully again till the bear disappeared into the brush.

Lily and JD brought a picnic lunch, and they ate near the creek, the gurgling sound of the water a sweet accompaniment to his son's chatter. Carter insisted on time for a nap back at the mansion before the full night they had planned— the harvest festival for Thad, hopefully much more for Carter and Erin. Though Thad protested, he piled up on the couch opposite Carter with a book, and they both fell asleep for a bit, Carter after long minutes of watching his son, content and flushed with fresh air and sunshine, snoozing with a half-finished copy of *The Lightning Thief* forgotten on his stomach.

When Carter woke, it was to his phone buzzing on his belly.

> Erin: Dad brought my truck over. Gonna run back to the house for a shower. Meet you guys at the festival?

> Carter: Definitely. And Erin?

> Erin: Yeah?

> Carter: Be sure to bring an overnight bag. Oh, and wear lace.

He was grinning at his phone like an idiot when JD came in. "You two gonna snooze the night away?"

Thad stirred on the love seat. It took no more than a second for him to register JD's words and he was jumping to his feet, book forgotten. "Is it time to leave?"

"We've got a little time to get ready," Carter told him.

"Why don't you run upstairs and clean up? It'll probably be late when we get home, too late for a bath."

"Dad…"

Carter held a hand up. "Don't forget to wash behind your ears."

Thad frowned, but a lifetime of experience had taught him that Carter wasn't giving in. As he ran for the stairs, Carter called, "And brush your teeth while you're at it!"

Thad's grumbling could be heard until the bathroom door shut. JD chuckled. "Times like these I wonder what kind of parent I would have made. Not nearly as good as you, I believe."

Carter wiped a hand down his face. "Not in the cards for you and Lily?"

"We've talked about it a little, but the possibility that Lily would take that step at this point is unlikely. She's been happy without kids all these years, and now, with the risks at our ages… It's just not for us."

"Nothing wrong with that." Carter yawned so big his jaw popped. "You certainly get more sleep without kids. That's an important factor when you're middle-aged."

Carter created air quotes around the hated phrase, and they both made expressions of disgust. JD sighed. "No doubt."

Carter's phone buzzed again.

Erin: Blue or peach?

The images immediately popped into his head, and Carter's hands shook as he replied.

Carter: Peach.

"Erin?" JD asked.

Carter set his phone down. "How did you know?"

134

"The silly grin on your face."

Carter rolled his eyes before getting serious. "So…would you be upset if Erin spent the night tonight?"

JD's eyes went wide. "Are we already at the spending-the-night stage?"

"And if we are?"

JD blew out a breath. "Well, you're adults, so okay." He rubbed a hand along his jaw. "Want me to set up another room? The one next to yours is free."

Carter couldn't hold back a grin. "Definitely."

"So what does this mean?"

That was the question, wasn't it? "Right now it means we want to get to know each other better. After that…" He shrugged.

JD shook his head. "All right, man, but don't be surprised if it ends up meaning a lot more than that. Lincoln and I both thought we were safe, and now look at us."

The idea would have disturbed Carter a few days ago, but now? What was that Erin had said to him earlier?

He thought he might just be looking forward to it.

CHAPTER
Nineteen

Downtown Black Wolf's Bluff was notoriously packed every year for the harvest festival, but parking had been arranged at some local stores—Walmart, a grocery store, the Presbyterian church—to allow bussing to the area. Erin met Thad and Carter at the Piggly Wiggly and boarded a yellow school bus with twenty other eager couples and their kids. The bus let them out at the courthouse just as dusk was settling. The temperature had dropped about ten degrees from its already cool state, but bundled in their coats and gloves, knit caps on their heads, the three of them set out for the ticket booth before beginning the night at a two-story bouncy slide Thad was practically drooling over. The kid was so darling in his excitement that Erin had to forcibly stop herself from scooping him up and smothering him with cuddles like that little girl in *Despicable Me* who just wanted to squeeze her unicorn plushy to death, he was so cute.

They were walking toward the line when Erin felt a gloved hand surround her own. She startled and stared down at Carter's fingers clasped around hers, trying to comprehend the fact that she was holding hands—in public

—with Carter Deveraux. The infamously grumpy Carter Deveraux. And yet a thrill ran through her at just his touch through both of their gloves. And when she glanced up, it was into warm blue eyes smiling down at her, not a grump in sight.

As they waited for their turn on the slide—and yes, Erin was willingly going down a two-story slide, all for the pleasure of a cute little boy—Big Rich lumbered up and thrust his huge hand out at Carter. "Willard! I'm Big Rich. Own the Casa Blanca off Highway 20. Great to meet you!"

Carter's mouth opened, but nothing came out.

"Dad?" Thad's little brow was wrinkled with confusion. Erin barely resisted the urge to crack up.

And then Carter came to the rescue. He grasped Big Rich's meaty paw and gave it a hearty shake. "Nice to meet you too, Big Rich. This is my son, Thad."

Thad gave Carter a side-eye but shook Big Rich's hand with the dignity of an adult.

"I've known our Erin since she was a tiny thing. It's good to know she's caught her a good'un." Big Rich leaned close. "You are a good'un, aren't you?"

Thad immediately came to Carter's defense. "My dad's the best."

Erin's heart melted. She put an arm around Carter's waist. "Of course he is," she assured Thad, "but I appreciate your concern, Rich."

The line moved forward, forcing them away, and Big Rich gave them a satisfied nod as he walked on. A few seconds passed before Thad tapped Erin's hand where it still rested on Carter's waist.

She peered around Carter. "Yeah?"

"I thought Willard was the peacock. Why did Big Rich think that's my dad?"

That was all it took to get past her control; Erin immediately burst out laughing. This time it was Carter giving the side-eye, but the one-sided grin on his face said he could see the humor in the situation.

When Erin finally got herself under control, she attempted an explanation. "So...Lily and I might have led Big Rich to believe I had a fake boyfriend as an excuse not to get roped into a date."

"With Big Rich?"

Carter snorted.

Erin took back her arm and elbowed Carter in the ribs. "No, with his nephew."

Thad thought about that as they eased forward. "That's kinda how you make excuses not to go on the dates Aunt Emma tries to send you on, Dad. But you don't need a fake boyfriend for that."

"I certainly hope not," Erin said. Carter looked sheepish. Leaning around him again, she told Thad, "It was just a little joke between Lily and me."

And the rest of the town, apparently. Word had gone from Big Rich to everyone else; every booth they stopped at, someone would introduce themselves to "Willard" and be sure to mention how good it was to see "our Erin" with someone steady. Erin thought her teeth might crack from gritting them, but the guys played along, never once giving a hint that Carter was not, in fact, Willard the Peacock.

Even Linc got into the game when they arrived at Gimme Sugar's booth. Much to Erin's—and Thad's—amusement, the famous chef and his fiancée were dressed as pirates in flashy old-world costumes. Linc even sported a gold ring in his ear that Erin secretly thought was incredibly sexy. She eyed Carter, imagining his hair long enough to curl, combined with that close-cut beard, the serious expression, and a flash of gold in one ear. He must've interpreted her look correctly because he gave her a frowning shake of his head in return.

She pouted to express her disappointment.

"Well, hello, *Willard!*" Carter's friend called as they approached.

Carter grumbled under his breath.

"What was that?" Linc brought a hooked hand to his gold-decorated ear. "I couldn't hear you over all the squawking going around."

"I'm not the one *strutting* around, proudly displaying his feathers," Carter said, pointing to the black feather sticking out of Linc's hat.

Claire laughed. "There is only one man around here that's as proud as a peacock."

Linc scooped her against him and nuzzled his nose into her neck. "And I have every right to be."

She swatted him playfully. "Wanna decorate a cookie, Thad?"

While Thad chose a pumpkin sugar cookie from the array of options and moved down the table toward the orange icing, Linc kept up his teasing. Erin abandoned the two men in favor of helping Thad with piping and sprinkles.

"Those two are crazy," Claire said.

"They certainly are. Carter has let the entire town believe he's Willard."

"And Willard's a peacock," Thad proclaimed, seeming as proud as one of the notorious birds to be in on the joke.

Claire laughed. "I've met him," she told Thad. "He's not as nice as your dad."

"Definitely not," Erin agreed.

Claire gave her a knowing look. "I think we need a girl's night so you can fill me in on what's going on. I've been too busy with the festival preparations and Linc being here to get the latest gossip."

"I'm sure we'll have time tomorrow night when you come up to the mansion." Erin offered Thad the purple sprinkles to go on his pumpkin cookie, noticing the boy had a smear of orange icing on his cheek. "Looks like someone is decorating himself as well as the cookies."

Thad laughed, swiping the icing from his face and sticking it into his mouth.

The two of them shared the finished cookie as they moved on. At a far corner lot, they ran into her friend Scarlett and Iris Daniels, the town's head librarian. The two women were manning the costume booth, dressed in flashy red saloon girl costumes with crisp crinoline layers to lift their skirts and sexy leather boots. Erin oohed and aahed over their attire while Thad and Carter took advantage of the double row of hanging costumes. They ended up in pirate outfits that were almost as awesome as Linc's—minus the gold earring, unfortunately—and Carter added a couple of massive feathered fans in honor of his alter ego when the two had their picture taken together.

Needless to say, Scarlett and Iris were almost as taken with Erin's companions as Erin was.

They grabbed hot dogs at a nearby street cart; then next up came the petting zoo. As they approached, Carter leaned close to Erin, his breath warming her neck when he whispered in her ear, "Now that's a great costume."

Erin eyed Farmer MacDonald—yes, that was his name—standing at the entrance to the petting zoo. The man had a massive round belly that he'd covered in an old flannel shirt and ragged coveralls that strained at the middle. Muddy boots on his feet. A grizzly brown and gray beard that fell almost halfway down his chest. A straw hat protected what she knew was a mostly bald head, and the pièce de résistance was the thick piece of hay sticking out of his mouth. She turned to Carter.

"That's not a costume. That's how Ol' MacDonald always looks."

Carter's mouth dropped open.

Thad, of course, heard her. She was learning that he heard pretty much everything.

"Is his name really Ol' MacDonald?"

At least the child had discretion down pat; he kept his voice low.

"His last name is MacDonald, and I guess officially he's Farmer MacDonald," Erin told him. "But we've called him Ol' MacDonald since I was a kid."

"How old is he?" Carter asked out of the side of his mouth as they approached the gate.

Erin smirked. "No one knows."

"Erin!" MacDonald gave her a bear hug in greeting that felt like it might squish her bones. "I heard you were here with some company." He gave Carter a polite nod before turning to Thad. "Who's this handsome fella?"

Thad introduced himself, of course. The kid had never met a stranger. MacDonald gave him a firm handshake and took the time to introduce him to his pet llamas, Laurel and Hardy, before returning to the gate.

Thad seemed to be in heaven with all the animals. There were baby goats bopping around, bouncing off hay bales and each other like kamikaze daredevils. A sleepy calf that chewed contentedly as children ran their hands over his soft neck. Baby piglets that squealed in their pen, some fat and pink, some creamier with brown and black spots. There were even a couple of ponies that meandered around, their quiet eyes taking in the chaos with barely a blink. At one point Thad sat in some straw to pet a couple of puppies, and a huge chicken clucked right up to him before settling itself in his lap. While Carter snapped pictures on his phone, Erin explained that Rhode Island Red chickens were extremely friendly (though she'd never met one quite this friendly) and showed him how to pet the deep orange-red feathers on the bird's back.

The haunted house was next. The guided tour allowed

them to warm up inside, and just as Erin had hoped, Thad loved the decorations and even seemed to enjoy the stories read in each room. Carter waited until they reached the backyard before easing her into a dark corner, away from the crowd, pulling her close, and whispering in her ear, "I have a newfound appreciation for haunted houses."

He was kissing her when Thad discovered them a few minutes later. Oddly enough, Carter's son didn't say anything about what they were doing; his grin seemed to say it all.

Hot chocolate (sugar-free for Carter) warmed them up on the way to the final side of the square. Thad was visible flagging, but he perked up as they approached the post office. Lou Rutledge, their resident postmistress, had gone all-out for the festival, including sporting bright orange as her chosen hair color tonight, along with a deep purple witch's costume complete with broom. Snookums, her cat, sat beside her on his leash, his orange coat set off by his matching purple bow tie. The cat blinked pretty green eyes up at Erin and meowed before ambling over to greet her. Much to Thad's delight, the cat not only rubbed all over Erin's legs but sat nicely for Thad to get in some pets.

"Oh, Snookums loves our Erin," Lou bragged, watching the cat indulgently.

Carter, snuggled up behind her, chuckled, the vibrations transferring to her through their coats. "Everyone has a thing for you, don't they?"

She winked at him over her shoulder. "Why wouldn't they?"

His look was hot, even in the moonlight. "Indeed."

Thad and Erin played cornhole. Thad won a small fox stuffed animal, but Erin went a bit further and had her choice of the biggest offerings. Eyeing the toys, she finally chose a big, floppy brown bear and handed it over to Carter when she rejoined him. "To remember the Smokies by," she told him.

The bear was half as big as him. "How am I supposed to take this home on a plane?"

She just laughed. "Let Thad use it as a pillow."

And that was how they made their way back to the Piggly Wiggly, with Carter on the window side, Erin tucked against him, and Thad laying his head on the big fat bear in her lap. When they reached the parking lot and got off the bus, Carter kept hold of her hand, his other one urging Thad and the bear he was hugging along until they reached his SUV. He got Thad into his seat, told him he'd be right back, and locked his son inside before walking Erin to her truck.

"You'll meet us at the mansion, right?"

Erin unlocked her truck and opened the door. "If you're sure that's what you want."

Carter took her face in his hands and tilted it up for his kiss. A long, wet, thorough kiss. The scratch of his beard against her skin reminded her of that same sensation in other places.

"It's definitely what I want," he said.

"I'll be there then." She got into her truck, cranked it, and waited till Carter's SUV was moving, then followed him out of the parking lot. She didn't stop smiling all the way out of town.

CHAPTER
Twenty

To give Carter privacy to put Thad to bed—and avoid any awkward questions—Erin said good night when they arrived, then followed Lily into the kitchen for a nightcap. Thad was, as predicted, too tired to do more than pee and brush his teeth before crawling onto his air-mattress pallet with a yawn that threatened to rival a lion's. He even skipped the usual protest of Carter returning downstairs to be with the other adults. Carter's good night received a mumbled response, and he was pretty certain Thad was asleep before the door was firmly closed behind him.

Downstairs JD, Lily, and Erin congregated in the living room with cold bottles of beer. JD passed him a frosty glass of ice water. "Sit down, bro. Claire and Linc should be here soon; they're wrapping up at the bakery."

As much as he appreciated that the three of them were rarely in the same town at the same time anymore, a confab with his brothers was not how he planned to spend the night. Plus they had tomorrow for all the talking they wanted. Tonight, every second he could squeeze out would be spent with Erin—in bed.

"Thanks, but we're beat. Wrangling a ten-year-old around

a fair is exhausting." It wasn't a total lie—all the excitement had been tiring, but not too tiring. Not enough to make him bypass Erin in his arms. He grabbed the water with one hand and Erin's hand with the other, pulled her up from the couch, and ignored Lily's amused pout and JD's flat-out laughter in favor of hurrying Erin toward the stairs.

"Well, that wasn't awkward at all."

Thank goodness she laughed when she said it, or he'd have been sadly disappointed. "I'm fine with awkward if it means I get you naked sooner," he said, keeping his voice down as they passed the door to his and Thad's room. The next one over shared the bathroom between them, and with the door on Thad's side left open, Carter knew he would hear his son if he needed him even with the door on their side closed. And locked.

"I'm not going to argue with that."

Anticipation tingled down his spine to his balls with Erin's words. Every physical encounter with Erin up to this moment had been satisfying, but he wanted more than quick sex—he wanted to lay her out on the bed and take his time, give her more than the one or two orgasms she'd had so far. He might be tired, but he'd stay up all night if he had to. Opportunities like this didn't come around often.

They entered the bedroom. Carter glanced around, grateful to see JD or Lily had provided plenty of bedding for them. He locked the door behind them, then crossed to the bathroom door, made sure the night-light was on, closed that door as well, and flipped the lock.

"Thad?" Erin asked softly with a nod toward the bathroom.

"Yeah." He set his water on the dresser and stalked toward her, shedding his sweater along the way. Let it drop to the floor behind him. "We'll have to be quiet."

Erin likewise set her half-empty beer on the bedside table and began to take the pins out of the loose bun she'd had her hair in beneath her hat. "Quiet might be a problem," she teased, eyes glinting in the sparse light from the bathroom and the one outside, overlooking the drive, that filtered through the blinds.

His shirt came off next. "It will be if I have anything to do with it."

Erin's hands lifted to meet his chest as he stepped close. "I can tell you're a runner." Her gaze devoured him. When she traced a couple of small bruises on his belly, one brow lifted.

"Injections," he told her. Insulin pens didn't usually leave marks, but occasionally he'd get a little circular bruise.

"Hmm." Fingers sifted through the sparse hair on his pecs, circled his nipples, drawing a sharp gasp from his lips. "Such beautiful muscles."

He clenched his hands on her hips and threw his head back, reveling in the slow burn of pleasure her touch ignited. "I'd rather see your muscles than mine."

She flicked a nail over one hardened tip. "Would you now?"

"I would." He reached for the hem of the red sweater that complemented her coloring so well, and drew it up, up, up, leaving her silky skin bare in the lightest of peach lace. The fabric cleared her head, and a growl escaped him.

Scratching her nails down his abs, Erin chuckled. "I bet I know something you'd like even more."

When she began to sink to her knees, his breath stopped. "Erin?"

The fact that his voice had dropped to no more than a rasp widened her smile. "Carter?"

He tore the button of his slacks open. Erin's laugh went deep, husky. And then there was no more laughing as she eased the sides of his pants open and peeled them down his thighs. His boxer briefs joined them. Erin's breath hit the head of his shaft, and Carter's knees gave out.

"Just a sec." The theme of tonight was taking their time, so he settled on the side of the bed, kicked the rest of his clothes off, then pulled Erin between his thighs. Staring down at her was like looking at a fallen angel—her thick brown hair floated in a cloud around her head, giving her a just-had-sex look. The curves of her breasts looked naked in the darkness, the lace blending in with the creaminess of her skin, the hard points of her pink nipples threatening to break through. And the look in her eyes…

That look alone would get her cast out of heaven. Sensual. Hungry. Desire darkened her expression, emphasized her full lips and the flush on her cheeks. He reached for her, threading his fingers in that beautiful hair. "Is this okay?"

Erin nodded, the slight tug tightening her expression, the hunger in her eyes burning brighter. "Yes." She licked her lips. "And this?" One fingernail traced up the back of his erection.

The thick length jerked. "God yes."

"Good."

She leaned in, her breath hitting his sensitive skin just before her tongue did. Carter moaned.

"Shhh."

The vibration of her warning against his cock had him arching, pushing his length closer to her mouth. "Erin…"

She licked the mushroom head.

"Erin…" This time his moan was even more tortured. Tightening his hands in her hair, he drew her forward until her open mouth sucked him in. He bit down on a shout.

The suction…God. Her mouth was magic, drawing on him as if he were her favorite meal. Taking him in, pulling back. The slide along his skin sent tingles through his sac, a warning that he wouldn't last long if she kept at him. He could handle that—he planned to play with her a long time, and getting off now meant more stamina later. Still, he wanted this to last, wanted to imprint on his mind the memory of her tongue stroking the veins of his cock, her wet heat surrounding him, making him think of a similar heat soon to come. She breathed through her nose, the puffs of air cooling his skin each time she retreated, her mouth heating him back up almost immediately. The dichotomy was driving him crazy, and he felt his fingers clench, felt his desperation rise the longer she sucked him.

"Erin…" His breath was nothing but pants, but he managed to get out her name—a warning. Those mysterious green eyes looked up at him, pleasure seeming to light them from the inside. God, so beautiful. "I'm gonna come."

She smiled around his cock, and a warning shot of precum left him. Erin licked at it, then backed off, let her hands take over to jack him to the end. Not nearly as good as her mouth, but he wouldn't force her to take his full—

"Shit!" The harsh whisper left him just as he shot come onto Erin's skin. Just the sight, that creamy expanse, the peach lace now coated in white, set him off again, then again. Erin worked him until shudders signaled the end, but he couldn't take his eyes off her wearing the evidence of his orgasm and how beautiful it was.

And then she kissed the tip of his cock.

He jerked. Another muttered curse had her grinning.

"Think you're pretty hot stuff, huh?" he asked, voice hoarse.

She arched a brow. "Oh, I know I am."

He groaned as an aftershock shot through him. "You'd be right."

She slowly stood up between his legs, casually letting those tight nipples brush against his skin. Carter released her hair and ran his fingers through the wetness on her skin, rubbing it in. Marking her. When it was all dry, he went for the clasp of her bra behind her back. It popped open with a flick of his fingers.

"You've got some moves of your own," Erin said, appreciation in her smile.

"You bet I do. Wanna see?"

Before she could answer, he had her nipple in his mouth, drawing on her just like she'd drawn on him. Hands firm at her back, keeping her close, he nibbled and sucked and bit, driving her into a frenzy as he switched from breast to breast, taking as much as giving. He'd always been a breast man, although Erin's ass and legs and pussy definitely got him going. But here, with her areola bright pink from his mouth and her nipple a hard little point against his tongue—he knew he could stay here all night.

"Carter," Erin hissed. "Please."

Reluctantly he withdrew. Stripping her tight jeans and lacy panties took no more than a minute, and then he was laying her out on the covers, baring her body to him in a way they hadn't managed to get to before. A huff of breath left him. "Damn, Erin." His fingers weren't quite steady as he traced up one long, long leg, across her flat stomach to her ribs, around one round breast to the tip, then up her neck. He gripped her chin in his hand and moved over her on his hands and knees. "You're a beautiful woman."

She moved restlessly beneath him, giving away her need.

He nipped her chin, traced back down her body, and took her mouth as he dipped his fingers inside her.

Erin bucked, her lips opening on a gasp. "Carter!"

"Shhh," he breathed. The invasion was gentle, slow, and he mimicked it with his tongue, taking her kiss, delving inside, exploring, feeling his way. She was dripping wet between trembling legs, her pelvis arching to urge him deeper, but he made her wait, made her endure the rising need as he played to his heart's content. Only when her nails were digging into his shoulders and she was raggedly whispering his name into his mouth with every thrust did he scoot down her body, take her pretty little clit between his lips, and suck her hard as the quick driving of his fingers brought her to completion.

Erin strained up, her body bowing as the sensations overtook her. Long seconds later she flopped back to the mattress, her breath heaving. Sweat glistened on her skin, and her breasts shook, tempting him again. He sat back on his feet and palmed her mound, allowing the pressure to bring her back to earth.

But he wasn't done.

As Erin rested, eyes closed, he took her hands and brought them to her breasts. Her eyes popped open.

"Play with them for me."

He waited, wondering if she would do it, praying she would follow where he led. Her nipples had softened with her orgasm, probably still sensitive, but Erin flattened her palms and began rubbing them gently, slowly bringing them back awake. He watched as he gripped her legs beneath her knees and raised them up and out, allowing him to scoot his body right up against hers.

Erin gasped when she felt his hardened cock at her core. Her hands clenched mounds of sweet flesh.

"Easy," he breathed. Angling his shaft, he centered himself and began a firm push into her body. "Easy."

But Erin didn't struggle away; instead she widened her legs farther, opening herself completely to his invasion. The feel of her, bare and wet, a tight clasp surrounding his cock, had his eyes rolling back in his head.

"So good, Erin." He bottomed out, then held himself still, giving her time to adjust. "You feel so damn good."

She moaned, arched her body up his bent legs to push him deeper into her. "So do you."

His erection thumped inside her.

Erin grasped her nipples between her forefingers and thumbs. As he watched, fascinated, she began to pinch and pull, far harder than he would have dared. He caught the rhythm, beginning with tiny pushes to open her back up, then slightly harder thrusts. His fingers got busy between her legs, tracing her open lips, the place where his body entered hers, the shy clit back under its hood. Slowly he coaxed it out with tiny circles of a wet fingertip. Erin's breath picked up, her body mimicking his in-and-out motion, making it more forceful, driving herself onto him and forcing both of their needs higher. Watching her spread out for him, her body bare, her face alight with a desire that had him thrusting even harder inside her, was...incredible. It was the only word that came to him. She was incredible.

And to think he'd almost lost the chance at this by being a stubborn jackass.

The thought brought a groan to his lips. He leaned forward onto his knuckles, pushing hard, thankful this bed had no headboard or he'd be alerting the whole house to the driving depths of his need as he slammed hard against her. The move caught her clit between them, and Erin gasped his name. Tiny spasms clamped down on his cock. Pulling one hand away, he leaned even farther and took a nipple between his lips.

One suck was all it took.

Erin clamped her free hand over her mouth to stifle the wail that left her as she plunged over the edge. The hard pulses took him with her. He couldn't slow, couldn't stop, could only force himself tighter and tighter against her as both of them lost themselves in the oblivion only the other could provide.

He had no idea how long they lay there in the aftermath. When his brain finally came back online, he stood and moved to the dresser where he'd stashed a damp rag and some towels earlier. Erin's eyes opened as he walked back to the bed.

She didn't stop watching him as he cleaned her up, cleaned himself. He tossed the cloth onto the floor and stretched out full-length beside her. The kiss he gave her was gentle, sweet—enough, for now.

Then he placed his hand on her lower belly, right above her womb, and pressed down, waking her up once more to the sensations he'd given her.

"Again."

It was going to be a long, long night.

CHAPTER

Twenty-One

Erin was sound asleep when Carter woke the next morning. From the angle of the sunlight against the blinds, he figured it was about eight—not surprising given how little sleep they'd gotten. Wanting to allow Erin a bit more rest, he eased out of the bed, slid on his boxer briefs, and exited through the bathroom door.

A quick shower washed away some of his fatigue, and anticipating the coffee that would help even more, he dried hastily and went into his and Thad's room to dress and take his morning insulin.

Thad's palette lay already empty. Carter threw on warm clothes and hurried downstairs to catch up with his son.

The other two couples were eating at the kitchen table— French toast and bacon, it looked like. The room was redolent with the scent of maple syrup and salty meat. Carter's stomach rumbled. "Where's Thad?"

"He's eaten and gone outside already," JD said around a bite of bacon. He chewed and swallowed. "Don't worry. I made sure he was wearing shoes and warm clothes and his coat"—he counted off on his fingers—"and warned him to stay in the backyard."

Carter raised a brow. "But did he brush his teeth first?"

JD gave a mock groan. "I knew I forgot something."

Carter beelined for the coffeepot, shaking his head solemnly. "And I thought I could trust you."

"Hey, you could trust him to keep the secret of where you were sleeping," Lily said. "We told Thad you'd already gone for your run."

The flush he felt in his cheeks was probably just the heat rising off his coffee, right?

"Want some French toast?" Linc asked.

"Would love some." Carter took a couple of sips from his cup, then set it on the counter and headed for the back door. "You get started and I'll check on my son."

He hadn't considered that Thad would wake up before him and wonder where he was. He was such an early riser, and Thad had always been a good sleeper. Guess JD had saved his ass with that one.

The French doors opened onto a cool but bright morning. Carter scanned the back patio but didn't see the sturdy ten-year-old body or thick curls of his son. Calling Thad's name, he headed around the side of the house. He'd allowed Thad to roam pretty freely as long as someone knew where he was. Since he'd been told to stay close—and there was no Erin to sneak off to visit—Carter assumed Thad was somewhere around the periphery of the house.

Five minutes later, a quick search and regular calling showed no signs of his son. Still, Carter wasn't too worried. He jogged up the hill to check Erin's shed. All was quiet. The build site was silent this weekend with the town festival to occupy everyone. Keeping an eye out, Carter ran back to the house, going inside without a glimpse of Thad.

"JD." He was breathing a bit heavy as he entered the kitchen.

"Plate is ready," Linc said.

Carter held up a hand. "I can't find Thad. Can you help me look?"

"He's not in the yard?" Lily asked, rising from her seat.

"No."

Carter turned to go back outside just as Erin reached the bottom of the stairs. One look at his face and her soft smile faded. "What's wrong?"

"I can't find Thad."

"Did he go up to the shed?" she asked.

"First place I checked," Carter said, shaking his head. "I'm going to look again."

Erin nodded. "I'll grab my shoes and join you."

The adults checked all the obvious spots once more. When no little boy appeared, and no evidence that he'd gone up or down the hill, Carter began to truly worry. "Thad!"

"Thad!" JD echoed at the other end of the yard, then Linc out front.

Lily rushed through one of the back doors, her face frantic. "Carter!"

He hurried over. "Yeah?"

She gestured him inside. "Come see this."

His heart was still racing with the realization that his son could be anywhere on this mountain. It sped up even more at Lily's words. He followed her inside, vaguely aware of the others doing the same. In a small alcove under the stairs, a hidden door stood open. Inside Carter could see what looked like the security system and a video screen.

"I checked the security cameras," Lily said. Carter let out a hard breath. "I rewound to when Thad went outside. Look."

Carter looked. The camera was on a spot to the right of the French doors, the images running in fast-forward. On-screen, the door opened and Thad entered the yard. For a few minutes all was normal—Thad jumping around, climbing the tree at one corner of the patio, picking up sticks and stacking them together in different shapes for his own amusement. It wasn't until about ten minutes passed that anything unusual happened. Thad was playing some made-up game involving the sticks at different intervals and running around them in a pattern only he understood; then suddenly he glanced toward the woods and came to an abrupt stop.

Lily slowed the replay. Carter broke out in a sweat. God, not the woods. "Is it a bear?"

From behind him, Erin's hands settled on his biceps and squeezed.

"I don't…" JD leaned closer. "I don't know."

They must have all seen it at one time, because a collective gasp arose. There, just at the edge of the woods and barely discernible on the fuzzy black-and-white screen, was the vague outline of a deer.

Carter sagged in relief. Not a bear.

As they watched, Thad stared at the animal as if fascinated. Carter would have been too, still would be now if terror wasn't gripping him as Thad eased closer to the animal.

"No, son. Don't."

But Thad did. He followed the animal as it eyed him warily and retreated into the woods.

Into. The. Woods.

"I'm calling Papa," Lily said. Carter was vaguely aware of a phone call commencing as he watched Thad advance into the woods, farther and farther, until his navy-blue coat became a blur among the trees and brush and then was gone.

Thad. Carter realized he was hunched over almost as if he'd taken a punch to the gut. He straightened. "I've got to go find him."

"We're not gonna have all of us lost in the woods," JD said firmly. "Henry knows what he's doing. Let Lily talk to him while we get ready to go."

Carter looked down, realizing he had on shoes with no

socks, a long-sleeve shirt with no coat. He knew he needed more, but the what wouldn't come to him.

Erin tugged at his arm. "Come on. We'll gear up, and by then we should know what to do."

He and Erin put on socks and boots, warm coats and gloves. In the sun it was merely cool, but the woods were all shade and much chillier. Thank God Thad was wearing his coat.

Back downstairs, Lily had two backpacks filled with whatever Henry had told her to prepare. She handed a thick pocketknife to JD. "Erin, you have yours, right?"

Erin patted her cargo pants pocket. "Always."

"Mark a tree every few feet with a distinct gash on the trunk, or break a branch on a bush if no trees are nearby. That way you can track your path back out." Lily pointed. "Water, snacks inside. I don't have space blankets or whistles, but I included a throw in each pack in case you find him. Claire and I will stay here. Papa is calling the sheriff, and they'll be here soon." She looked Carter in the eye. "I figured you wouldn't wait."

"No way in hell."

She held his gaze firmly. "You have one hour to come back. Beyond that, we have to get the professionals, understand?"

He nodded. And so they set out. Erin and Carter entered the woods where Thad had and tried to take as straight a path as possible. Lincoln and JD headed downhill. Carter noticed Erin setting a timer on her watch, and then she drew that sharp pocketknife out and flicked it open. While she marked, he called for his son. For a few minutes he could hear his friends doing the same, but gradually their voices faded as the woods absorbed the sound. The realization had his heartbeat stumbling over itself.

He kept calling, paused every few minutes to listen for Thad's response. About twenty minutes in, he and Erin took a short water break. "What if he doesn't answer?" he asked Erin.

"Then like Lily said, we get the professionals in here." She cupped his cheek, rubbing her thumb over his short, thick beard. "Believe we'll find him first."

And he tried to. The longer they called, the more he worried. The half hour mark came, and though Erin urged him to return, he stubbornly refused. They could go back faster when they weren't looking for Thad; another fifteen minutes wouldn't hurt.

Erin was arguing with him at the fifty-minute mark when he swore he heard a sound that wasn't her voice. He lifted a hand. "What was that?"

Erin went silent.

Nothing.

"Thad! Thad, answer me!"

He held his breath, waiting, and then, faintly, he heard a sound. It echoed in the air.

Shit. "Which way?" he asked Erin.

"Keep moving forward." She dug her knife into the nearest tree. "And keep calling."

Carter did. A minute passed, feeling like an hour, and then he caught sight of movement up ahead.

Small arms waving in the air. Navy-blue covered arms.

"Thad!" He ran then. Thad's head jerked up at his call, and then he was running too, straight for Carter. They met halfway, Carter scooping Thad into his arms and heaving with tears as he held his son close.

"God, buddy, I was so worried."

"I'm so sorry. I'm so sorry, Dad!" Thad was crying too.

Carter cuddled the small body to his chest, rubbing his arms up and down Thad's trembling back. Hushing the shaky apologies. The story tumbled from Thad's lips—how he'd seen the deer, how he'd followed. How he hadn't even realized he'd gone into the woods until the deer spooked and bounded off, leaving Thad alone and scared. He'd been so scared he'd run blindly, no idea where he was going, until he'd had to stop to rest and Henry's words about being lost in the woods had returned to him. *Hug a tree*, the man had said. So Thad did. He hugged a tree, waited, and believed his dad would come.

And Carter had come.

When they both began to calm down, he realized Erin hadn't just been standing by. Her phone was in her hands—she was texting. Telling everyone they'd found Thad. Now they only had to make their way back to the mansion and this little misadventure would all be over.

Thank God.

A fifty-minute walk holding a ten-year-old wasn't easy, but Carter refused to put Thad down. And Thad refused to let go. Only, the closer they got to the edge of the woods, the worse Carter began to feel. His shaking had subsided as they searched for Thad, but now it came back quickly. His head began to pound. Nausea rose in his throat. He stumbled, thinking he should really let Thad walk, but his fingers refused to release him. And then he saw the edge of the woods and the tree that sat next to the patio.

They were back.

The three of them broke through the trees. Before his vision blurred out completely, Carter saw the others rushing toward them, and then he was on his hands and knees. "Thad!"

Erin must have turned back to them because he sensed her there, picking Thad off the ground, the urgent tone of her voice trying desperately to break through the fog that had taken him over. He barely heard her over the dry heaves that shuddered through him. The shaking he couldn't seem to stop. He wanted it to stop, needed it to stop, but he couldn't seem to get his body to cooperate.

Next thing he knew, he was on his back, staring up at the

clear blue sky. Erin's face hovered over him, Thad's next to her. They were calling his name—he could see their lips moving, though the sound didn't register. His heart was pounding out of his chest, and he tried to tell him, but the dark rushed in, stealing his ability to move.

And then there was nothing.

CHAPTER
Twenty~Two

E rin heard a distinct thud behind her, mingling with
Thad's alarmed cry. When she spun around, she saw
Carter on his hands and knees, one palm pressing
against his chest, head down. Thad lay on the ground
beside him.

Everything inside her froze. It was like time reversed
years in a single second, and all she could see was Stephen on
his hands and knees, gasping out some of his final breaths on
this earth.

"No!"

She was beside Thad, picking him up off the ground, with
no idea how she'd gotten there. The sounds of Carter dry
heaving and Thad crying filled her ears.

Carter rolled onto his back. His eyes rolled back in his
head.

"Carter!" She leaned over him, her gaze centered on his
face. "Carter!"

His eyes closed.

"Dad?" Thad skirted Carter to lean in on his other side.
"Dad?"

That was when the convulsions started.

Terror shot through her. "Carter?" She glanced around frantically. "JD!" Oh my God.

JD ran up to them and dropped to his knees at Carter's head. "Shit!" He yelled over his shoulder, "Lily, call an ambulance!"

"Thad, move back," Erin said, wanting him safe. Not wanting him to see his dad die.

Thad shook his head. He leaned down, his face near Carter's head, far enough away that Carter's jerking body wouldn't hit him but close enough his words registered in Erin's ears. "It's okay, Dad. It's okay."

"Thad—" No, this couldn't be happening. "Carter." She reached for him.

"No!" Thad slapped her hand away. "Keep back. He's okay."

He definitely wasn't okay. "His heart—"

"It's not his heart," JD said as the jerking of Carter's body continued. "It's his blood sugar."

What?

Thad murmured words as close to Carter's ear as he could get, but Erin noticed the tears streaking down his cheeks were fresh, not from earlier. Her fists clenched around limp grass and crispy fallen leaves. "Thad…"

Linc leaned over Carter's legs, a hand on his friend's thigh. Erin was vaguely aware of others around them, but her brain wouldn't register who they were. She watched as Carter's body stilled, eyes closed, the tension in his muscles seeming to seep away.

Oh God, was he— "Carter!"

"He's okay."

How the hell could JD sound so calm? Erin tore her gaze from Carter and noticed JD's fingers on his neck, checking his pulse. Thad reached across his dad's body. "We have to turn him—"

Carter's body went board stiff again. Another seizure.

"Go look in his room," JD barked at Linc. "He should have sugar tabs. Or grab some juice."

She knew for a fact Carter wasn't swallowing anything right now. Even juice.

JD must have noticed her confusion. "For if he wakes up," he explained.

"I don't understand. What's going on?" she asked.

Thad was the one who answered. "His sugar's too low."

The words were logical, and on some level it registered that Thad must have seen this before, but she also noticed an edge of hysteria in the boy's words. So did Lily, she guessed, because her friend knelt beside Thad. Not touching—Thad seemed too intent on Carter for that, too tense—but giving him the comfort of another human being close by.

Carter calmed again, his body going still. God, she couldn't believe she was thinking of him as a body.

At Carter's head, JD gripped his shoulders and heaved. Automatically Erin assisted, and with everyone's help they got Carter onto his side. JD shucked his coat and shoved it below Carter's ear to keep his head steady. "We just need to get his sugar back up."

Erin tried her damnedest to follow JD's words, but her brain kept flashing back to Stephen and those awful last moments of his life. When Claire wrapped an arm around her shoulders, she realized she was crying.

Lily had a hand on Thad's back. "He's gonna be okay," she murmured. "The ambulance will be here soon."

"Did he take his meds this morning?"

Erin glanced up and realized the man speaking was Sheriff Fowler. Henry Easton stood behind him. They were supposed to come to help find Thad, she remembered now.

"I don't know," JD responded. "I know he didn't have time to eat before..."

The words trailed off, but Erin saw him glance at Thad. The boy must have caught the meaning of his words, because he curled onto the ground beside his dad as sobs began to leave him. "This is my fault."

Lily moved closer. "No, absolutely not."

Erin knew her friend's words wouldn't help, though. Not for a while. She couldn't have prevented Stephen's heart attack, but she'd lived with the guilt of not doing so for years.

At least Carter would be alive to help his son get through it.

The sound of a siren rising up the mountain reached her ears. A few minutes later, Linc rounded the house with Colby Reeves and another man Erin didn't know, both wearing the navy shirt and dungarees that were the uniform of the local fire department. Colby was a nurse and fire department volunteer. He carried a medical bag while the other man pushed a stretcher through the rough grass.

Lily urged Thad to his feet. "Let's give them some room."

They all backed away, JD staying close to give Colby the details of what they knew. Colby went to work fast, checking Carter's vitals, and by the time the stretcher had caught up to them, they were ready to lift Carter onto it.

JD came around to Thad's side. "Do you want to go with him?"

The boy blinked wide eyes, his curls wild around his head. "Uh-huh."

Sheriff Fowler looked on sympathetically. "They can only take adults."

Erin's spine straightened. "We'll follow along behind, then. Come on, Thad." She gestured him toward the house. "I'll get my keys and we'll be ready by the time they have your dad in the ambulance."

Thad didn't argue. And just as she'd said, by the time she'd retrieved her keys and they'd gotten back out to her truck, Carter was in the ambulance. She got Thad buckled in, and the two of them set off down the mountain, right behind Carter.

"He's gonna be okay. He's gonna be okay."

From the corner of her eye Erin could see Thad rocking in his seat as she drove. She wished she had words of wisdom to make him feel better, but unfortunately her wisdom said that would take a while. But finally she could stand it no longer.

"Thad? Thad?" She waited until he turned to her, his eyes meeting hers briefly. "Do you want me to call your mom?"

He seemed to consider that for a moment. Finally he shook his head. "I want to see my dad."

"I'll have us there as soon as possible." But she wanted him to be prepared. "I don't know how long we'll have to wait before they let us see him though."

Thad frowned but didn't argue. Which made Erin wonder...

"Has this happened before?"

"No." Thad looked out the window. "But I've been to classes. The teacher told us what to do if Dad got really sick."

"Because your dad is diabetic."

"Yeah. Dad's real careful about his medicine, but"—he shrugged—"he says accidents happen."

Accidents happen. How true that was. She wasn't sure how she felt about a ten-year-old being prepared for a medical emergency like that, although Thad had handled it way better than she had, she guessed.

"JD and Linc will come to the hospital soon," she tried to assure him, assuming the familiar presence of his "uncles" would help.

"But you'll stay with me?" he asked.

Her heart melted into a puddle at his words. "I'll stay with you. Every single second," she promised.

She pulled into the ER parking lot while the paramedics unloaded Carter. When she and Thad arrived at the registration desk, they were directed to wait as Erin had expected. Lincoln, Claire, Lily, and JD arrived shortly after. JD got Rachel, Carter's ex-wife, on the phone and, after explaining the situation, handed the cell to Thad so they could speak. And all the while, Erin tried to ignore the flashbacks of Stephen's last moments stuck on replay in her head.

Lily sat beside her and reached for her hand. "I guess coming here isn't pleasant, huh?"

She took in the waiting room consciously for the first time since they'd arrived, realizing they were back in the hospital Scott had been brought to. The hospital Stephen had died in. "Yeah."

Lily squeezed her hand. "You okay?"

"Me?" She shook her head. "Of course."

Her friend leaned closer. "There's no 'of course' about it."

Erin sighed. "You're right. I feel so…just… I don't know."

"Shock."

"Probably right again." Tears thickened her voice despite her attempted chuckle. She needed to stay calm, clearheaded, not cry. And yet… "Why do I keep ending up back here?"

"Erin—"

"You know Carter would never ask that of you."

She glanced at JD in surprise. Of course Lily would have told him about Stephen. She frowned at him. "Carter didn't have to ask anything of me. Neither did Thad. I'd be here regardless." She straightened her shoulders. "I don't abandon people I care about. For any reason."

"That's you, Erin. Always fixing things."

Her stomach tightened at Lily's soft words. "There are too many things that can't be fixed, Lily. We just make do and move on."

"I don't think that's the case with you at all, my friend." She scooted closer to Erin and pulled her into a side hug. "I think you're always so busy fixing things for other people, taking care of them, that you sometimes forget to take what you want into consideration."

Erin glanced over at Thad a few seats down, still on the phone with his mom, and longing squeezed down on her heart. Was that what she wanted? Thad and Carter and a family of her own? Because that was impossible. Her business was here. Carter's life was in New York. And even if his business was movable, Thad wasn't.

Lily frowned. "Hey." She reached up and wiped away a tear Erin hadn't realized was on her face. "It's all right. There's nothing wrong with caring about other people, Erin."

Except caring meant hurting; she knew that from past experience.

"Deveraux family?"

She looked toward the nurse waiting at the double doors to the ER.

"Erin?"

Thad had hung up the phone and stood, waiting expectantly for her. Because she'd promised.

"I'm coming." She swiped away her tears and stood. "Let's go see your dad."

CHAPTER
Twenty~Three

C arter woke the first time in the ambulance. A redheaded guy with a full beard told him what had happened, which explained why he felt like shit. He wasn't surprised, though. He worked hard to stay healthy and stable, but this morning his focus had been solely on finding Thad, not on making sure he ate. A lot of people assumed diabetes was only about avoiding high blood sugar, but the opposite could be just as dangerous.

The paramedic had assured him Thad was following them to the hospital. Knowing that, he let exhaustion take over and slept for the rest of the journey. And again after the initial fuss of retaking his vitals and getting an IV in.

The next time he woke, it was to a warm, slight weight on the bed next to him, cuddled up to his side. The scent of antiseptic and the beep and whoosh of various machines reminded him where he was, why he was there, but when he raised a hand to investigate, the IV line restricted his movement.

"Dad?"

Thad scrambled to sit up at Carter's side, worried eyes the same color as his staring down at him.

Carter lifted his unencumbered hand. "Come back here." He needed to feel his son in his arms, know he was truly here and not lost out in the woods somewhere. Only as Thad lay down against him once more did he feel like he could take a full breath. "I love you."

The most important three words in the English language. He said them to his son often, but now… A tingle told him tears weren't far off.

"Love you too, Dad," Thad whispered against his shoulder.

"I'm sorry I scared you. Are you okay?"

Thad shook his head hard against Carter's shoulder. "I wasn't scared."

Carter might have believed that if his son's face wasn't buried against him, his small hands gripping Carter tight. "I'm gonna be fine, all right? My body's just tired. I'll need some extra sleep, but I'm okay now." Having your sugar drop too low was exhausting. He'd known that from past experience, but nothing could have prepared him for how bad it felt to hit rock bottom.

"He's been telling me that the whole time," a feminine voice said from the other side of Thad. Erin stood and rounded the end of the bed to stand beside him. "He kept telling me you'd be all right. He's been a real trooper."

He searched her face, trying to read the experience through her eyes, see just how bad it had been—for Thad and for her. "Guess we've put you through the ringer this morning, huh?"

Erin shrugged. "That couldn't be helped. The two of you are both fine now; that's what matters."

He wasn't sure that was true. It wasn't every day he scared a woman he'd just slept with by trying to die on her, but hopefully it hadn't traumatized Erin too bad. The compassion in her eyes as she stared down at them together on the bed gave him hope.

The doctor deemed him stable midafternoon, and Erin took him and Thad back to the mansion. Only then did she leave, saying she needed to check some things at home but that she'd be back for the fire that night. Linc fed all of them hearty snacks, and then Thad and JD began a rummy tournament around the living room table to keep Carter company as he slept the rest of the afternoon.

Not exactly how he'd expected to spend their last day of vacation, but they were both safe and sound, so he'd take it.

Because the sun set behind the mountain, dusk came early to the mansion. Around five thirty JD wrangled Thad into helping him find kindling for the fire. They scoured the yard for a tidy heap while Linc moved logs from the woodpile to the large fire pit JD had installed for the fall. Lily set up a ring of folding chairs, and Claire arrived just in time with an SUV full of food that could feed an army. She unfolded a table near the circle to hold all the food and condiments, paper goods and utensils, and even had these nifty little umbrellas made from netting that kept any bugs from getting into the food. When Carter saw how she'd labeled each of the items that she'd made sugar-free so that he would know what was safe for him to eat, he gave her the biggest bear hug—until Linc told him to knock it off or he'd be eating coal instead of homemade marshmallows tonight.

So Carter retreated to his seat with a diet soda and watched his friend teach Thad the best way to build a fire, starting with the kindling.

"So we've found something he's good for besides cooking?" JD asked.

"Fires are good for more than cooking pizza, I guess," Linc said archly.

"I thought that's what the microwave was for," Carter threw in.

Their chef friend growled.

The sound of a truck engine signaled Erin pulling through

the gate, and Carter felt his heart do a little flip in his chest. She joined them just as the fire took off, blazing high above the pit. "Wow, are we having a campfire or a bonfire?"

Thad giggled. "Uncle Linc says we have to build up the coals first."

"He's not wrong," she said. Glancing around, she noticed Carter in a blue hammock seat, and immediately settled in the one next to him.

"Drink?" JD asked.

"You bet."

"Any driving tonight?"

Carter held his breath. Erin paused as if she didn't know how to answer. Taking that as answer enough, JD nodded. "Nonalcoholic it is."

Disappointment settled in Carter's gut. And then determination. This was his last night here, and he wanted Erin with them. With him, all night long.

They spent the next few hours roasting hot dogs and marshmallows over the fire, eating and drinking and laughing. Carter had missed being with JD and Lincoln, but he found he didn't resent the addition of the women. In fact, having Claire and Lily and Erin with them just enhanced everything. And of course Thad entertained them all.

At one point, when everyone was distracted by Linc's impression of a chipmunk with marshmallow-filled cheeks, Carter leaned close to Erin.

"You've been awfully quiet tonight."

When she turned her head, she brought them nose to nose. "Have I?"

He wasn't sure he'd ever get enough of those mysterious moss-green eyes. "You have." He wasn't certain if it was the aftermath of a very long day or if she was pulling away from him or if it was something else, but whatever it was, he wanted to know. He didn't want her to pull away from him.

"I didn't mean to be," she confessed against his lips.

"Good." He closed the last few centimeters between them and took her mouth. She tasted like sugar and spice and Erin, and it was the Erin part he liked best.

Finally, a moment of real connection with her. He hadn't realized how badly he'd needed it until that moment. And he wanted more, a lot more.

Reminding himself they weren't alone, he eased back.

"Mmm." Erin licked her lips. "You taste good."

"Funny, I was just thinking the same thing about you."

"Dad! Look at the bunny I made!"

Marshmallow ears stacked on a s'mores bunny were pretty impressive, but Carter regretted the loss of intimacy with Erin. A few minutes later when things were quiet again, he asked, "Can you stay?"

Erin looked down at the ground. "I don't think that's such a good idea. You really need to rest, Carter."

"Then you can rest with me. Just…stay."

She stared at him in the firelight for a moment; then a hint of amusement tipped up the corners of her mouth. "Okay."

Since it was their last night of vacation, Carter let Thad stay up a bit later than usual, but finally it was bedtime. Thad complained—and Carter understood, but he also needed some time alone with Erin. After getting Thad showered and tucked into bed, he got himself cleaned up, then gave Erin her turn in the bathroom. A quick peek assured him Thad was asleep. Carter breathed a sigh of relief and escaped into the other room.

When Erin exited the bathroom, Carter was already beneath the covers. Despite the sleep he'd gotten all day, sinking into the mattress beneath warm covers was pure bliss. As was seeing Erin cross the dim room toward him. She was clothed in the Henley he'd given her last night, thin enough to drape softly across her braless breasts, and soft boxers that left her long legs bare to his hungry gaze. His fingers itched to take the clothes off her, to explore even more than what they'd gotten to explore last night, but Erin was right—with a two-hour drive to Nashville and a long flight home tomorrow, he needed to rest.

That didn't mean he couldn't enjoy her being beside him.

As she lifted the covers to crawl into bed, he raised one arm. "Com'ere."

No protest. With a soft smile, Erin crossed the wide mattress on her hands and knees, scooted her body right up against him, and laid her head on his shoulder.

Warmth. Woman. He wanted this to last.

Maybe forever.

"Are you all right?"

Erin huffed, reminding him that though she could be soft, she could also be tough as nails. "Shouldn't I be asking you that?"

He reached up to brush her hair back from her face, giving him a clear view. "Care shouldn't be one-sided."

She ran her fingers across his chest. "You're right." A pause. "Today was rough."

He sighed. "It was. I'm sorry to put you through that."

She gave him a light smack. "Don't apologize to me. As if you could help it."

He chuckled and clasped her hand, protecting himself from any more retaliation.

Another pause. The silence was loud in his ears, but he waited Erin out.

"Today brought up a lot of memories that I'm still struggling to process."

He squeezed his eyes shut. "Memories of your husband?"

He wasn't jealous. Even if he'd wanted to be, he'd slap that shit down. Erin didn't deserve to deal with that. She'd loved her husband; he knew that much. And his death had hurt her deeply. But she also wasn't pushing people away because of that. Hell, she'd even given him a chance at a time when she'd have been totally justified in pushing him as far away as possible.

"I saw Stephen die," she finally said, her words barely more than a whisper. Her fingers clenched in his chest hair. "I rode in the ambulance with him to the same hospital you were in today. I was holding his hand when he took his last breath, in a bed in the same ER."

He cursed under his breath. "I'm so sorry." He had moments of his own, from his own marriage, that he still remembered starkly—not the least of which was the moment his ex-wife had admitted she was cheating. But that kind of devastation was nothing compared to what Erin had endured.

Erin flattened her hand out, returning to her earlier petting. "That's the problem with living in a small town—you can't run away from the memories. In some ways that's good, because you don't forget the good things. But that also means that sometimes the bad things get brought up, through no one's blame, and you sort of have to sift through it all over again. Sometimes that is easier…"

"And sometimes it's not," he finished for her.

"Yes."

He turned carefully onto his side, pulling Erin closer. His legs tangled with hers, their bellies touching, her breasts, free from her bra, mashed against his ribs. He kissed her softly on top of her head, drawing in the unique scent of her. The scent he was coming to love. "Then let me hold you through it," he said. "I don't need to take anybody's place, but I'm not going to leave you alone either. Just let me hold you."

And that's what he did for the rest of the night.

CHAPTER

Twenty~Four

They were both awake far before dawn. Erin could feel Carter thinking even if he didn't say anything. *She* should say something, but she was afraid anything she said might put him off, so she kept quiet and tried to enjoy the novelty of being held for once.

Of course, if she could sense him, she should have guessed Carter could sense her.

"You're thinking so hard you woke me up."

His voice was gravel-rough in the mornings. The tone sent a tingle down her spine. What would it be like to wake up to that sound every morning?

"I think that was the other way around," she joked. "Your brain works really loud."

Carter chuckled. He'd stayed close all night, but now he curled tightly around her back. Spooning. It felt so good.

"So what has you thinking so hard this morning?" she dared to ask.

"Your husband."

She jerked in his arms, not because she wanted to get away, but because the answer shocked her so much. "Stephen?"

"Yes."

Again with the thinking. She sat up carefully and turned to face him. The windows were just lightening up, enough that she could see the frown lines between his eyebrows, around his mouth. She reached out to smooth them away. "Tell me."

"I don't know a lot about your husband's death, but...I haven't been able to stop thinking about what you told me last night. I guess..." He drew her hand away from his face and brought it to his mouth for a kiss. "I guess I need you to know that if we were together, I don't expect you to be my caretaker. I've been taking care of myself for years. I've never had a medical emergency like I did yesterday. It wasn't intentional."

"I'd never believe it was, Carter." He wouldn't risk putting Thad through that.

"It never would have happened if I hadn't been so focused on finding Thad."

She squeezed the hand that held hers. It seemed she wasn't the only one needing reassurance. "I do understand that." She took her hand back—and his—and kissed his palm. "I never had to be Stephen's caretaker. His death was a surprise to all of us. But yesterday..." Now it was her turn to frown. "Memories of the kind of pain I experienced when Stephen died don't just disappear into thin air. They ease with time, yes, but they're always there, imprinted on your mind. And I wouldn't be smart if I didn't think about it seriously before getting involved with someone else who could leave me like he did. Do I want to go through that pain if I lose someone I love again?"

Carter sucked in a breath, held it. Sitting up, he propped himself on his hands behind him. "Do you? Want to get involved with me, I mean?"

That was the million-dollar question, wasn't it? The one

she hadn't been able to get off her mind since they'd gotten to the hospital. Did she want to get out now, before she really got attached?

Who was she kidding? She was already attached. She couldn't call it love, not after a mere seven days, but if she'd lost Carter or Thad yesterday, the pain would've left a huge scar on her already scarred heart.

"I have to be honest with you, Carter: I don't know if I'm ready to love again. Not right now. We spent half of this week fighting."

His grin was a little crooked, a fact that his beard mostly hid, but she could see it now. "We did."

She grinned too but then got serious again. "So, I don't know if I'm ready, but what I do know is that I want to find out." She reached out to smooth the sleep-mussed lines of his facial hair. "I feel something for you, something I can't yet put a name to, but it's there. Is that enough for you?"

He leaned in, his mouth going to the smooth line of her collarbone to place a gentle kiss. "It's more than enough for me."

Tension drained out of her in a rush. "Oh thank God. I thought you were going to make me sweat that one."

"No way." He nipped the bone just under her creamy skin. "I want to get laid before I leave you today, and making you sweat any other way wouldn't work in my favor."

"Oh really?" She reached for him, dragged her hand down his pec, came to his tiny nipple standing at attention…

And pinched.

Carter yelped. Then fell back onto the bed, one hand over his mouth to try to keep the sound of his laughter muffled.

Taking advantage, Erin crawled over him to settle herself on his lower abdomen.

Carter stilled.

"Is this okay?" she asked.

"It's more than okay." His voice had gone back to that gravelly tone. "I don't think I've seen much that comes close to how beautiful you look right there."

His words sent warmth shooting through her. She was a simple country girl, she knew. She'd never been out of the South. Lived most of her life on a farm. She'd always thought about herself as sturdy, not beautiful. That this definitely beautiful, sophisticated man thought she was made her melt.

"And Erin?"

"Yeah?"

"I care about you too."

"Thank you." He didn't have to give her that, but she was glad he had. She reached for the hem of her shirt. "Now what was that you said about getting laid?"

He definitely got laid. Twice. Once there in the bed, and then again in the shower, though that one had to be quick and as silent as they could make it, given the proximity to Thad's room. Still, Erin was feeling satisfied and deeply refreshed despite her lack of sleep when she went downstairs to see about breakfast. She should have known Lincoln would already be on it. Watching the man put together a frittata and fresh biscuits was like watching a magician work magic.

"I think if you're going to be part of the family, you need to give cooking lessons," she told him.

Linc smirked. "If I can get my schedule under control and be here more often, you got it."

"I'm sure Claire would love for you to be around more."

"And not for the cooking lessons," JD called as he walked into the kitchen.

Linc jerked his head toward the counter. "Fix the coffee?"

JD got to work, and in minutes they had breakfast on the table. Erin poured coffees and handed them over to be customized or not, as the recipient desired. Carter and Thad arrived, and Carter beelined for the coffee.

"Black, right?"

Carter hummed against the rim of his mug. "Like to keep it pure."

She laughed. "I like a little coffee with my cream and sugar."

Carter shuddered.

"That's how I like my coffee too," Thad said.

"Is that so?" Erin reached for another cup.

"Oh no you don't," Carter said. "That's all we need is you bouncing all over the plane once we get aboard."

Thad pouted, but the sight of biscuits a second later seemed to distract him and he hurried toward the table.

They ate and talked, all of them together except Claire, who'd had to be at the bakery early this morning. After breakfast, Erin and Lily cleaned up while JD helped Lincoln, Carter, and Thad get their luggage packed into the SUV. Lincoln was hitching a ride with Carter to get to Nashville, though his plane would be headed for California instead of New York City.

All too soon it was time for the guys to go.

Linc gave Erin a quick hug and moved on to JD and Lily. When she turned to Carter and Thad, whom she was beginning to think of as *her guys*, she was, thankfully, alone.

"I guess it's time," she said.

Carter stood, his hands firm on Thad's shoulders, his smile sympathetic. "We'll find a way to get back to see you," he said.

Thad dropped his bear stuffed animal and threw his arms around Erin's hips. "It feels like we just got here."

And in that space of time, her life had changed. Cuddling Thad to her, she knew it had changed for the better. She could already see herself being part of this little family. But letting go now, especially with things so new, was going to be hard.

"I guess you've got to return to school," she reminded

Thad. "But you'll be back in December for the wedding, right?"

The words wobbled the slightest bit, and she prayed Thad didn't notice. When she glanced up, she knew Carter had.

"He can't miss the wedding," Carter said. "He's the ring bearer."

Erin sagged in relief.

"But you can always come see us in New York," he said quietly.

The thought sent her heart into her throat. Go to New York? Could she survive New York? She'd never been farther north than North Carolina. But scared or not, she'd do it for them.

Them. Not just Carter. How had this ten-year-old boy managed to worm his way so deep into her heart?

"Buddy"—Carter picked up the bear and dusted him off —"we've got to get a move on so we don't miss our flight."

Thad sniffled. Erin didn't mention it, but she did squeeze him tighter before letting go. "I'll see you soon, Thad."

He nodded, head down. "Okay. Bye, Erin."

"Bye."

Carter put Thad in the SUV, the bear in his lap, then closed the door firmly. Wrapping an arm around her waist, he urged her toward the back, giving them a degree of privacy. His kiss was hot, intense, and flavored with her tears.

When Carter released her mouth, he brought his thumb up to caress her wet bottom lip. "We'll figure this out, Erin, okay? Don't worry."

"I'm not going to worry." She tried to smile through the emotions churning in her belly. "If I matter to you, you'll make the effort. And I will too."

"Then we'll succeed." He swooped in for one more kiss, two, then stepped back. "I'll see you soon."

He continued around the SUV and got into the driver's

seat. Erin stood back, watching, as the trio took off. She watched as they drove through the gate, and listened to the sound of the engine all the way down the mountain.

Carter's words came back to her. *We'll succeed.*

God, she hoped he was right.

CHAPTER
Twenty-Five

Erin: Guess we better get used to this, huh?

Carter: As long as text doesn't become an excuse not to call. I don't want to go days without hearing your sexy voice.

Erin: I don't think anyone has ever called my *voice* sexy.

Carter: Get used to it. I think all of you is sexy.

Carter: How do you feel about sexting?

Carter: At a family dinner but wishing I was talking to you instead.

Erin: Emma still hasn't given up?

Carter: My sister is insane. Will not leave me alone about dating. Claims "Erin" is the name I gave my blow-up doll.

Erin: You have a blow-up doll?

~

Erin: Not feeling so hot today.

Carter: You're always hot.

Erin: Ha ha *green-faced nausea emoji*

Carter: That bad?

Erin: Yeah. Going back to bed. Call tonight? I want to talk to Thad.

~

Carter: I only had you in bed for two nights. How can I already hate sleeping alone again?

Erin: I thought Erin the Blow-up Doll was keeping you company.

Carter: A blow-up doll could never compare to being inside you.

Erin: Carter!

Carter: What?

Erin: … … … I miss you too.

~

E rin had been up at dawn feeling sick, which was how she realized her toilet was leaking before it flooded her bathroom. A couple hours of work and then she got to go in to her actual job. None of the guys were in a good mood either—it was Friday and everyone just wanted to go home.

Her phone buzzed in her pocket midmorning.

Carter: What are you wearing?

Erin: Dirty overalls.

Carter: What color is the lace underneath them?

Erin: I'm standing 5 feet from 10 sweaty guys who are wondering why I'm blushing. Don't do that!

The three bouncing dots appeared, telling her Carter was preparing a reply. The string of emojis he sent next took a minute to interpret, but when she did, she blushed even harder.

Erin: Carter!

Carter: You send me that text a lot.

Erin: You earn it a lot.

This time it was the laughing emoji with tears coming from its eyes. She sent back an eye roll.

Erin: I think I got myself involved with a pervert.

Carter: I think you love that about me.

Erin: Yeah, I kinda do.

How could his texts make her feel happy and sad at the same time. Still moping later in the afternoon, she took out her phone and reread their last few messages. Four weeks. Just four weeks since he'd been gone, but each day had felt like forever. Carter was right; they'd had two days of sex, been in each other's physical presence for a total of only seven days. How could being alone already feel this empty?

She was convinced now more than ever that what they had was worth pursuing. Hell, she could even admit to herself that she was in love with him. She just had no idea how to overcome the obstacles that blocked the path to their being together.

Glancing around the shed, she felt a sudden swamping fatigue overcome her. Maybe she was depressed. Or just tired. Friday afternoon on a jobsite meant everybody cleared out as early as they could, and today, she decided, that was going to include her. A nap was just the thing to make up for her short night. Without stopping to talk herself out of it, she gathered her things and headed for her truck.

The clock had just hit four when she pulled into her driveway, and by five after she was piled on the couch with a blanket and a pillow in her comfy pj's. The pleasure of being off her feet was instant. She was asleep the second her eyes closed.

Her dreams were of Carter.

When she stirred two hours later, a quick glance at her phone said there was a text waiting, but this one was from Ruth. Dinner was ready—or had been thirty minutes ago. Groggily she sent a quick response, splashed some cold water on her face, then made the trek across the yard to Ruth and Scott's house.

"Sorry I'm late!" she called as she pushed through the door. Thank goodness Ruth had cooked or Erin would probably have ended up with a bowl of cereal for dinner. But the minute she walked inside, the overwhelming scent of collard greens cooked with ham hock slapped her in the face.

Oh no.

Erin skidded to a halt.

Ruth came through the dining room doorway. "I left you a plate in the microwave, Bug."

She swallowed hard. "Collards?"

Ruth nodded enthusiastically. "And cornbread, black-eyed peas, ham steaks. You ready to eat?"

With every item listed, Erin felt more and more nauseous. She swallowed once more, struggling to contain it, but when Ruth opened the microwave door and the scent of collards got even stronger, she knew the effort was fruitless. "'Scuse me!"

She made it to the bathroom just in time.

A while later—Erin wasn't certain how long she'd sat there with her head hung over the toilet bowl—she heard Ruth outside the door. A quick knock sounded. "You all right in there?"

She didn't know about all right—she was beginning to think something was seriously wrong with her stomach. Could she face the smell in the kitchen, that was the real question.

"I'll be out in a minute."

Avoiding the kitchen altogether, Erin took the long way around to the dining room. When she sneaked a glance through the doorway, she saw that the table was clear of any dishes. Thank God. She walked through.

Ruth watched her, concern etched into her expression. "Scott had to go out and close the door on Willard. He finally decided he was ready to go in to roost."

Erin nodded. Taking her usual seat, she plunked her elbows onto the table and rested her face in her hands.

"How long have you been sick, Bug?"

"I don't know," she mumbled into her palms. "It comes

and goes. I thought it would be better this afternoon since I took a nap, but I guess not."

Ruth was quiet for so long that Erin dropped her hands to look at her mother-in-law. "What?"

Ruth tilted her head. "When was your last period?"

Erin gasped. "What?" Why would Ruth ask her that? Yes, she'd been having problems with her periods before, but not now. Now things ran like clockwork...

She thought back a few weeks.

Oh. Oh no.

Five little words. All it took was five little words and her world went reeling.

"Erin," Ruth asked, obviously feeling her way through her words, "is there a chance you might be pregnant?"

Erin spluttered. Of course there wasn't. "I'm on birth control pills."

Ruth laughed gently. "Honey, I've known so many kids who were conceived while their mamas were on birth control."

"But..." Erin shook her head. "But..."

"Maybe think about that." Ruth reached across the table and patted her hand. "You wait here and I'll get you some crackers."

Erin did nothing more than stare into space until Ruth returned. The ginger ale and saltines helped settle her stomach but not her mind. "Oh my God, Ruth. What if..."

Ruth raised an eyebrow. "What if, what? You're pregnant? Then we're all going to be ecstatic."

"But Carter—"

"Hmm. Yes, Carter." Ruth cleared her throat. "Maybe you should find out for sure first. Worry about Carter then."

Oh, she definitely needed to make sure first. She stood so fast she almost knocked her chair over. "I'm going to run to the store. I'll be back." As she was running out the door, an idea occurred to her, and after checking in with her stomach, she called back over her shoulder, "I think I'll stop and get some fries." That actually sounded good. "I'll see you tomorrow, after the collards have disappeared."

"You better call me before then!" Ruth yelled after her.

"Yes, ma'am!"

Where should she go to get a test? No way in hell was she going to the local pharmacy where everyone who came in would know her. She drove to the next town over, Redwater, and stopped at a chain drugstore there. Her hand shook when she finally chose a pregnancy test from the ten different options available, but she managed not to drop it until she got to the counter. The older woman who checked her out gave her a benevolent smile and a wink as she took the bag and headed out the door.

Redwater also had a McDonald's, which was where she headed to next. A large fry and a chocolate shake were soon in her hands. It tasted like ambrosia, especially after feeling sick so often lately.

Well, duh. You should have figured this one out a long time ago.

We don't know anything for sure.

I think we do, but sure, let's take the test. Then you won't be able to argue with me. Yourself. Whatever.

Holy shit, what was Carter going to say?

She drove straight to Lily's house, thanking all that was holy that JD wasn't there when she arrived. She couldn't stop the nervous tapping of her foot on the front porch, the way the bag crinkled in her hand as she waited for her friend to answer the door. She was so anxious that when Lily finally appeared, she barged right through, nearly bowling her friend over. "I need some help."

Lily chuckled. "Of course. What do you need?"

Tearing open the bag from the drugstore, she pulled out the pregnancy test, whirled around, and held it in the air for Lily to see. "This."

Lily gaped. After a few long seconds—during which it

was obvious that Lily's brain was speeding along so fast it was practically smoking—she gave Erin a tentative smile. "Um, well…I don't think I can help you with that."

Erin looked at the test, then at Lily, then back at the test. She burst out laughing, then stopped when she realized she was on the verge of hysteria. "Not that kind of help."

"I figured." Leading the way from the living room into the kitchen, Lily went to the fridge and pulled out a pitcher of tea. "Want some?"

She was thirsty. "God, yes." Hopefully her stomach would tolerate it.

"Good." Lily shooed her away. "I'll pour; you go pee."

Five minutes later Erin walked back into Lily's kitchen, dazed. Lily took one look at her and hurried around the island to guide her onto a barstool. "You okay?"

How many times was someone going to ask her that? She was pretty sure she wouldn't be okay for a long, long time. "How could this happen?"

A little giggle escaped Lily's mouth. "Well, see…"

That did get a small smile. "Not what I meant." Erin rubbed a hand over her face. "I'm on birth control. I'm in my forties. This shouldn't have happened."

Lily shrugged. "Birth control is never a hundred percent. Lots of women are having babies in their forties now. Whether or not this should have happened is irrelevant—it did happen. You're going to have a baby." Her voice went up an entire octave, and she shook Erin by her biceps.

"I'm going to have a baby." Saying it out loud jolted her— and woke her up from the daze. "I'm going to have a baby." A flutter of excitement started in her belly. She took a small sip of tea, hoping it would stay down. "What am I going to tell Carter?"

Lily took the barstool next to her and thought about that for a moment. "I don't believe a baby is a reason to get married. You should get married because you love someone, not because the baby forced you to. So the question really is, how do you feel about Carter?"

If she'd been a cartoon character, she was pretty sure little hearts would pop up all around her head. "I think I love him."

A huge grin took over Lily's face. "I knew it!"

Erin frowned. "But…he's already a father. He has Thad. What if he doesn't want any more kids? We didn't even discuss it." She hadn't even considered it a possibility.

"Discussion or not, it is what it is. He's going to be a father again. And you're going to be a mom."

This wasn't a dream; it was real. She was pregnant. "I can't talk about this on the phone. Maybe I could video chat with him tonight." Just the thought made her nausea lift its ugly head.

Reaching for her phone, Lily smirked. "I think we can do better than that."

CHAPTER
Twenty-Six

He hadn't heard from Erin all day. A Saturday, so she should have been home. She hadn't mentioned any big projects going on that would have required her attention this weekend. So where was she? His text this morning hadn't gotten a response. He'd tried calling at lunchtime, and still noth—

"Carter! Aye, Carter!" Snapping fingers appeared before his eyes. "You 'wake in there?"

He jerked back from the hand so close to his face and blinked. "What?"

Gavin clucked at him. "I've been talkin' out of my arse for five minutes. Don' mind me, though. Arsehole."

Normally you could barely hear the Scottish accent unless Gavin wanted you to, but right now his brogue was sharp. Carter shook his head. "I guess I zoned out. Sorry."

"What's gotten into ya?" He frowned, swirling his Macallan in its square cut-crystal glass. "Yeah, I crossed the feckin' Atlantic Ocean because of work, but part of me only wanted to check on ya." His partner stared him down, green eyes glaring. Not the green eyes he wanted to be staring into, though.

He missed Erin.

"Ya've been downright moody lately." Gavin considered that, his head tilted to one side. "It has to be a lass. Who did Emma hook ya up with this time?"

That he could answer. "It's not someone Emma hooked me up with, thank God. Which is probably why it worked."

"Ha!" White teeth gleaming, Gavin raised his Scotch whisky and toasted the mystery woman. "Good. Emma has terrible taste in women."

"Probably because she's not interested in them."

Gavin chuckled into his glass.

"It's Erin."

Eyes narrowed, his friend seemed to shuffle through his memory. Carter knew when he hit on it because his eyes went wide. "The lass ya needed to apologize to?"

"That one." Then he found himself spilling out the story of Erin and the past five weeks.

By the time his words petered out, Gavin's eyebrows were at his hairline. "What the hell is with this lil' town? Every time one of ya goes to stay, ya get hitched up." He got a thoughtful look on his face. "Maybe I need to go. Do ya have any idea how slim the datin' market is for someone our age who doesn't want a twenty-year-old?"

"I was letting my sister hook me up with women. I do have some idea how slim the dating market is."

Gavin laughed. "That ya do."

A waiter interrupted, noticing their need for refills, offering cigars. Harrington's was an exclusive smokeasy in the Flatiron District with an old-world aesthetic that Carter found soothing—usually, at least. Today he doubted anything could quiet the uneasiness inside him.

Looking over the proffered selections, he and Gavin both chose an Olivia Serie V Melanio and went through the ritual of lighting, carefully nurturing the smolder until the cherry was evenly lit and they could sit back, relax, and enjoy the delicate caramel flavor of the tobacco. It wasn't something Carter did often, but occasionally when Gavin was in town, they would visit. Today Gavin had insisted, and now Carter knew why his friend had brought him down here.

To talk.

He nearly rolled his eyes but refrained. Barely.

"I don't know, man," Carter said, squirming to get just the right fit in his deep leather armchair. "I just... I don't know exactly what it is about Erin, or maybe the more accurate description is that I can't limit it to just one thing. But I do know this: I don't want to be away from her. This month has been hell."

Gavin frowned at the tip of his cigar. "So what's the problem?"

What wasn't? Their chemistry, that was for certain. They didn't struggle with chemistry. And she was phenomenal with Thad.

Speaking of...

"Thad's the primary issue, I guess. If it weren't for my son, I'd simply pick up my business and move to Tennessee."

"That serious?"

"That serious," he confirmed. "And it's not like I can't do what I do anywhere I desire. My family is here, but I can fly up and see them anytime I want. But I can't move Thad away from his mother." Nor did he want to miss any of his son's precious childhood.

"And Erin's job isn't as easy to 'pick up and move' as yours?"

"She's a general contractor with her own construction company. Sure, she could probably do that up here, but she has commitments down there, including elderly family that she won't leave."

Gavin made a low sound in the back of his throat as he

puffed on his cigar. "That is a head scratcher. But if ya can fly to see your family anytime, isn't the opposite true?"

Carter focused on his cigar but lifted a brow in inquiry.

"Look"—Gavin crossed one leg over the other knee—"I get it; ya want a full-time relationship with the lass. But ya also want to do what's right for your son."

"Absolutely. Thad has to come first." And Erin would totally agree with that, he knew.

"Sometimes bein' a mature adult means ya have to accept a little less in order to make everyone happy. Ya want to do what's right for your son, so be here when he needs ya. The weeks he's with ya, you're in New York. The times that he's with Rachel, you're in Tennessee. Fly back and forth. Maybe talk about summer vacation with Erin. Fly her up here when she can get away from her job." He gestured with his whisky glass as if to say, *Voila!* "If the two of ya want to be together, ya make it work."

Of that he had no doubt; they wanted to be together. They might not have said the words yet, but he knew in his gut they were there. But was this the right plan? It wasn't ideal, but... He let out a sigh of relief.

Gavin whistled under his breath. "Now there is one sexy lass. And bonus, she's not twenty."

Carter instinctively turned to look over his shoulder and froze. "Oh my God."

"What?" Gavin sounded downright grumpy. "Ya've already got a female; ya can't call dibs."

"I most certainly can. That's *my* female."

Erin was standing in the doorway of the club, outlined by the weak November sunshine outside and the floor-to-ceiling windows stretching the entire expanse of the bar on either side of her. But this wasn't his Erin—this was a New York City version of Erin. Her dark hair fell in gentle waves around her shoulders instead of braids or a ponytail. A red silk sheath highlighted the curves of her body, the athletic slenderness, and it fell only to midthigh, emphasizing the long, long length of her legs. His gut clenched when he got to the end of those legs: she was wearing heels. He'd only ever seen her in heels once, at the Carousel, and even then he hadn't gotten a good look.

"Excuse me." He stood.

Erin's gaze swept the room, but his movement drew her attention and she zeroed in on him. Then she smiled, the look shy, tentative. He smiled too.

"Erin." God, she was actually here. He hurried across the room toward her.

"I hope this is okay with yo—"

He took her mouth, cutting off her words. She tasted tart, like cranberries and lemon and sugar. He couldn't get enough of that taste, of *her*.

Erin pulled back, the sweetest giggle leaving her lips. "I'm happy to see you too."

"You can't imagine…" His words were nearly a growl as his hands eased down her hips and dragged her closer to the part of him that was hard and waiting.

"Oh, I can definitely imagine." She tipped her head, gaze moving over his shoulder.

"Want to introduce us?" his partner asked behind him.

He'd forgotten about Gavin. Damn.

"Erin Jenkins, this is my business partner, Gavin Blackwood," he said without releasing her.

"Hi." Erin reached a hand around Carter's waist since he refused to let go of her hips. "Lily has told me all about you."

"Not Carter, huh?"

"We had much more important things to discuss," Carter muttered.

He could feel Gavin's arrogant smirk, the one his friend always used around gorgeous women. "He's afraid I'd steal ya away with my seductive Scottish accent." He laid it on thick for the last few words.

"That too."

"Don' be rude, Carter," Gavin urged him. "Bring yer woman over to sit down."

They walked back over to their corner, Carter putting Erin in his seat before grabbing a chair from a nearby table. "How did you get here?"

"By airplane."

Carter chuckled. "Not what I meant."

Her smirk said she knew that. God, it was good to be with her again.

"Lily. And Emma."

"What?" His sister? He rubbed the crease forming between his brows. "Please tell me she didn't call you Erin the Blow-up Doll."

"I can't tell you that."

Gavin's deep laugh filled their space. "Sounds like Emma."

Carter cursed under his breath. "I'm gonna kill her."

Erin relaxed back in her chair. "From what she told me, you say that to her a lot."

"She earns it a lot."

"Sounds familiar." Erin tapped a finger on her chin. "I seem to recall—"

"That was flirting."

She shook her head, laughing. "No, it wasn't."

Gavin was watching them like they were the most interesting ping-pong match he'd ever seen.

The waiter stopped by their table again. "A drink for the lady?"

"Yes…" Carter was just about to suggest Erin's usual, Jameson with cranberry juice and ginger ale, when she responded.

"Just a ginger ale, please?"

The waiter nodded. "Right away, ma'am."

Erin grimaced as the man walked away.

Carter took her hand. "What is it?"

"He called me 'ma'am.'" She said the word like she would if she was calling the waiter a prick. Carter snorted.

Gavin laughed. "Don' they use 'ma'am' in the South."

"Oh yeah"—Erin pushed the hair back from her face —"but it's just polite manners. It doesn't make you sound like you're sixty."

The men laughed again.

"Well, you don't look a day over thirty," Gavin said gallantly.

Erin grinned Carter's way and jerked her chin toward his partner. "He's cute."

Carter growled under his breath. "Would you stop flirting with my woman?"

Erin's eyes went wide. Surprise glittered there, but at what, he wasn't certain. Then a thoughtful look came over her face, and she leaned closer to him.

He met her halfway.

"Am I?" she whispered under her breath.

"Are you what?"

"Am I your woman?"

Something inside him settled into place—Erin. As if she were a part of his soul he'd been missing all this time and he'd finally found her. He reached up to take her chin between his fingers. "I want you to be."

As those moss-green eyes stared into his, they softened with something that made his heart pick up speed.

"And suddenly I feel like a third wheel."

Carter kept his gaze on Erin. "That's because you are."

The corners of Erin's mouth twitched up.

"Wanna go home with me?" He couldn't wait to get her alone. He was even more impatient to get her naked.

"That is the whole reason I came here."

"Good."

"Good."

"Good," Gavin said, picking up his Macallan. "Then I'll go back to my cigar. I hope to get to know you better later, Erin Jenkins."

"You too, Gavin."

Carter stood, pulling Erin up with him. "Let's go."

CHAPTER
Twenty-Seven

New York City was a kaleidoscope of sights, sounds, smells, and textures that overwhelmed Erin's senses. It was kind of like Nashville on mega steroids, and that was just the parts she had seen. Carter hailed a taxi outside of Harrington's in deference to her heels —for which she was supremely grateful because her feet were starting to get desperate—and they were on their way to his high-rise apartment. She couldn't imagine living here. She couldn't imagine raising a child here.

Might want to get used to that one, Erin. After all, their child would be a mix of town as well as country. She couldn't ask Carter to uproot his child in favor of *their* child. Nor did she feel like she could completely uproot herself from her home. But together they could come up with a solution that would work, at least for now. Who knew, she might even begin to like the bustle and noise of New York…eventually.

She'd expected a lot of white and chrome and glass in Carter's apartment, mostly because that was how all high-rise apartments were decorated in TV and movies. The walls, though, were painted a soft cream that was warmed by the sunlight entering through the floor-to-ceiling windows. The furniture tended toward a dark, masculine vibe that suited him. She caught a quick glimpse of dark cabinets in the kitchen and a hallway leading the opposite direction before Carter dragged her through a hall and into what she assumed was his bedroom.

He slammed the door shut.

Navy-blue walls, lighter bedding, brown and leather accents. And Carter standing in front of her, as intent as a predator with his prey. His hands held her face at just the right angle as his mouth descended.

"Mine."

The word was growled against her lips just before he took her kiss. She had to admit, she was feeling just as needy, just as hungry for him as he seemed to be for her. It had been so long since she'd felt his touch. His kiss was hard, opening her mouth, seeking her tongue, delving deep to mimic things she knew would come later. Her body softened against him, female to male, molding to the hard planes of his body as naturally as breathing.

The perfect fit. That's what the two of them were together —the perfect fit.

Carter drew back, his breathing harsh in the quiet of the room. "I need you, Erin."

She smiled. "Me too."

"Good." Taking her shoulders, he turned her around. Impatient fingers went to the zipper of her dress.

"We should probably talk."

"We most definitely should," Carter agreed. Cool air traced her skin as the zipper lowered. "In a few minutes."

She couldn't help laughing. "All I get is a few minutes?"

Carter slipped her dress over her shoulders, his chest warming her back as the material caught at her breasts. His mouth found the join of her neck and shoulder, nestling into that notch that sent shivers down her spine. "That's as long as

I'll be able to wait." He raised his hands to trace the lace covering her cleavage. "No red this time?"

She arched her back, pushing for more of his touch. Her nipples tightened behind the layers of material separating her from him, including the creamy lace cupping her. "Not for the lace, at least."

Red silk slid down her body, a soft whisper against her skin. Carter covered her breasts with his warm hands. She couldn't hold back a moan.

"I've missed you so much." He traced her rigid tips. "Missed this."

God, she had too. "Carter…"

The next thing she knew, the world upended—Carter picking her up in his arms. Seconds later she was laid out on his bed.

"Holy shit, Erin."

She preened a bit, arching her body to tease him. Gaze fixated on her breasts, Carter looked as if he was about to devour her.

She certainly hoped he was.

Raising one leg, she planted the tip of the high heel Emma had bought for her on his chest. "Off." His shirt, her shoes—didn't matter as long as something came off.

"Oh no." Carter took the heel in his hand, shaking his head. "These are staying on."

"Then get naked for me."

She was pretty sure a few buttons popped off his shirt as he tore it open. He didn't even bother dropping his slacks—a quick unbutton and the sound of his zipper lowering and then he stepped close to the bed. Fingers found her clit through the lace of her panties. "Erin—"

She closed her eyes as pleasure zinged through her. "Yes."

Carter groaned. "Need you ready."

She planted her heels on the bed, opening herself to him. "Feel how ready I am."

He slid his fingers down, finding her wet. Definitely ready. He muttered a curse.

Her chuckle was strained. "Please."

Carter didn't strip her. He simply tugged her panties aside and lined himself up. The touch of his most intimate skin to hers had her slitting her eyes open. He towered above her, it seemed, his broad shoulders filling her field of vision as he leaned over her to plant his fists on the mattress. "Are you sure?"

She tilted her pelvis, sliding herself along his rigid shaft. "I'm sure."

Angling his hips, Carter notched his cock at her opening and began a slow push inside. "God almighty."

All she could do was moan. He set up an easy rhythm inside her that quickly picked up speed, driving both of them straight to the edge. She pushed up to meet him, allowing him deeper, his fingers finding her clit and forcing her up, up, up to the peak far quicker than she had guessed she could manage.

And then she climaxed, clamping down around him. Carter shouted, the warmth of his release filling her inside, spurring her on to greater heights.

It took more time to come back to earth than it had seemed to take to leave it.

Carter stripped her naked and tucked her under the covers, joining her a few moments later. He chuckled. "That was…"

She pressed herself against him. "Yeah."

Warm hands began a slow massage up to her nape, down to the curves of her rear. There was something she needed to do, she was sure, but for the life of her she couldn't remember what it was. The travel, the sex…suddenly all she wanted was to sleep right here, cuddled up against the man she loved.

Her eyes popped open. Oh, that was it.

Carter lined his face up with hers on the pillow. Blue eyes

held green. "I really hope this means you've made a decision about us."

"I've made a decision about us. Have you?"

He kissed her, the faint taste of smoky tobacco and alcohol adding a masculine edge to the essence of Carter. "Erin, I love you."

Her eyes closed, soaking in the words. Tears tingled at the backs of her eyelids.

"Hey." Carter came up on his elbow. "You okay?"

She opened her eyes and took in the love staring down at her. "I love you too."

His kiss was warm, tender. He kept close, his mouth brushing hers as he spoke the words she hadn't realized she was desperate to hear. "I want you to be mine forever. I know it's fast and I know we live a long way from each other, but I believe we can work it out. I want us to work it out so that we can be together."

Relief hit hard. Yes, she'd hoped. Even felt certain she knew. But there was nothing like the actual words to put all her doubts to rest. "I want that too. I want to be yours. And I want you to be mine."

"Forever?"

"Forever."

Carter kissed her again. They talked through the afternoon, making plans for the future, figuring out what they could do now and what would have to be decided later. It was a few hours before the distraction of Carter's wandering hands, their desperate lovemaking and intimate words eased and Erin worked up the courage to say what else she needed to say. Fear tingled in her belly at the thought of speaking the words out loud. What if this wasn't what he wanted?

"Carter?"

His tongue traced over her breast.

"Carter?"

He pulled back just enough to glance up at her. His smile was the sexiest thing she'd ever seen. "Yeah?"

She took a deep, deep breath. Carter went back to tasting her.

"I'm pregnant."

He froze against her.

She could feel the shaking start deep inside. Her fingers clenched in his hair. Forcing herself to relax, she said it again. "I'm pregnant."

"What?"

It wasn't a sharp *what*. He didn't sound angry. She forced another breath. Glancing down, she met his confused look and prayed the third time was the charm. "I'm pregnant."

He didn't ask how this could happen, didn't question her again. Instead he stayed there, frozen, staring into her eyes. She could almost see the gears turning in his mind, his brain putting the pieces together until he turned his gaze on her belly. Slowly he pushed his way down until he was even with her stomach. His breath teased her as he leaned in and placed his forehead against her navel. "A baby?"

"A baby."

"Are you okay?"

Carter had been through this before; he would know it was risky at her age. "I'm perfectly healthy."

Fingertips traced her skin right above her mound. "And the baby?"

She ran her fingers through his hair. "So far so good."

He looked up at her then. "Are you happy?"

She couldn't stop the smile that broke over her face. "So happy."

That was when he smiled. It was like the sun rising over the horizon, spilling out light to warm the world. Warm her. "A baby."

"I didn't—"

Carter leaned in and placed a kiss on her skin. Reverent. Awed. "Thank you."

She gripped his head and tilted it up, stared deep into his eyes. "I didn't plan this. I really was on birth control."

He shook his head. "I don't think you planned this." His fingers were tracing over her skin, his hands cupping her lower belly where their baby was growing. "But sometimes fate knows what you need before you do. I know how much you love kids. I do too. I never expected something like this to happen, but I don't think I could have imagined anything better than you in my life and a baby on the way." He winked. "Even if I had to apologize to get it."

Her laugh was shaky, a little tearful. "I love you," she said again, needing him to be sure, needing him to know she was sure. "I think I have since the first time you apologized."

Laughing, he scooted up until he was face-to-face with her. Fingers delved into her hair. Legs tangled with hers, bringing them firmly against each other. "I love you too. Thad loves you." A palm against her lower back pressed her belly to his. His mouth trembled against hers, betraying the emotion shaking him. "We're going to be a family."

And then he made love to her all over again.

Epilogue

D*ecember 25th*

"Merry Christmas!"

"Merry Christmas, cutie," Erin told Thad, grinning as she joined him and Carter in her living room. The room was lit by the soft glow of lights on the Christmas tree and hanging in the windows, still dark as they waited for the rising of the sun in a couple of hours. Colorful balls glinted among the evergreen branches, and Carter had lit a fire in the fireplace while she made coffee. She hadn't had a Christmas morning with a child since she'd been one, but seeing Thad's face light up as he hovered around the Christmas tree lit something inside her as well.

Love.

She'd known love all her life, from her parents, from Stephen, from Scott and Ruth and her friends. But nothing had prepared her for the way she could love a child, especially someone else's child. She loved Thad so much her heart ached with it. And if she'd thought Carter was a good parent before, watching him raise his son over the past couple of months had confirmed her opinion again and again. Basically living in two places at once wasn't easy, but Carter did what he had to do to make sure he didn't miss the important parts of Thad's life.

Her own life had changed so much in less than three months. Sure, she still lived in the same place and had the same job, but there was a richness to her life that had been lacking for so many years. She'd met a man that turned out to be perfect for her, despite a rocky start. She'd gained a son. And in a few short but seemingly far-off months, she would have a child of her own.

Just the thought blew her mind.

"What has Santa brought you?" she asked.

Joining Carter on the couch, she watched as Thad began to ooh and ahh over the shiny red bicycle in front of the tree. Carter took his cup of coffee from her, then raised a brow at the remaining cup in her hand.

"Decaf," she confirmed. She was just now beginning to drink coffee again. The first few weeks of her pregnancy had been rough. Morning sickness was from the devil, she was certain, and she'd had plenty of experience with it, but finally she seemed to be having more good days than bad.

Snuggling up to Carter's side, she sipped her coffee and listened to her guys discuss learning to ride this coming weekend. Thad put on the red helmet that matched the bike, though it kept slipping over his eyes until Carter adjusted the straps.

"Hey, how about you grab the stockings and bring them over here?"

At his dad's words, Thad was up and running. The small fireplace mantel held three hanging stockings, one for each of them. Just the sight of them made her tear up. She hadn't decorated her cottage for Christmas since Stephen had died, preferring to spend her Christmas mornings at Scott and

Ruth's house, but those matching stockings were a signal for her, of family and togetherness and the future. Her throat closed and her eyes tingled with tears as she watched Carter and Thad eagerly unpack the contents of their stockings, finding candy and small gifts she'd spent a long time deciding on. She'd wanted today to be perfect, and so far she was getting her wish.

"Open yours," Carter urged her.

Erin stuck her hand inside. First came a box of her favorite truffles from Gimme Sugar. A gift card to download some new music. A necklace from Thad. Then another box that looked like it might hold jewelry, except it wasn't a rectangle like Thad's gift. This one was a square.

From Carter, obviously. Maybe a bracelet?

But when she lifted the lid and looked inside, it wasn't a bracelet waiting for her. Not even close.

Thad was bouncing up and down in front of her, his excitement barely contained. "What do you think, Erin?"

"Yeah, Erin," Carter asked, reaching for the box. He pulled the ring from its velvet interior, the square-cut diamond shining like a Christmas light in the glow from the tree. "What do you think?"

That was it, there was no holding back the tears she'd been on the verge of for the past few minutes.

Carter chuckled and pulled her close to kiss away her tears.

"Why is she crying, Dad?"

Erin gave a watery laugh. Reaching out blindly, she found Thad's wrist, grasped it, and pulled him into her lap. "I'm crying because I'm happy," she said, hugging him tight. "It's a girl thing."

"Oh." Thad still looked confused. "But you like it?"

"I love it." Turning to Carter, she had to ask, "Are you sure?"

Carter set his coffee on the side table, slipped off the

couch, and knelt at her feet. "I want you to marry me, Erin. I want us to be a family." His quick glance at her stomach told her he meant all of *us*, not just the ones here now. "Will you marry me?"

Thad looked back at her from his position on her lap, his lanky body putting his head even with hers. "Will you marry us, Erin?"

There was no hesitation in her heart. "Yes."

Thad kissed her cheek as Carter slid the ring onto her finger. Then Thad hopped up to investigate the presents under the tree, and it was Carter's turn to kiss her.

"I love you," he whispered against her mouth.

"You'd better."

He grinned. "You too."

Half an hour later the living room floor was covered in torn wrapping paper and packaging. Toys and gifts littered the rug. Thad was about to crank up his new video game when Carter called him over. "We have one more gift for you, bud."

Nerves began rattling in Erin's belly. They weren't quite at the three-month mark, the traditional time to tell others about a pregnancy if there was any risk involved. But her pregnancy, though considered risky, had been textbook from day one, and an early ultrasound to confirm that fact had been done just the day before. She and Carter had discussed it, and she knew in her heart it was time to tell Thad.

"What is it?" Thad asked, bouncing up from the floor.

Carter pulled an envelope from his robe pocket. "This."

Thad frowned. An envelope usually didn't signal an exciting gift, but a gift was a gift, so... He tore the flap open. Inside waited a small photo on slick white paper, maybe three inches by four. He squinted down at it.

Carter took one edge of the image and pointed at the middle. "Do you know what this is?"

Thad shook his head.

"This"—he traced his finger over a white shape inside a black circle—"is the very first picture of your baby sister or brother."

"What?"

Erin swallowed hard, fighting the surge nausea rising inside her. Surely her morning sickness wouldn't return right at this moment.

"We're going to have a baby, son. Me and Erin. And that baby will be your brother or sister."

Thad's eyes went wide. He stared down at the ultrasound image, his finger coming up to trace the edges of the baby's shape just as Carter had. "Really?"

"Really."

Erin cleared her throat. "What do you think, Thad?" she asked hoarsely.

Without warning he threw himself against her, his thin arms circling her neck, his head burrowing into her neck. The sound of crying tore at her, and she looked at Carter, feeling helpless.

Carter rubbed his son's back. "It's going to be okay, bud. You'll love having a little brother or sister, I promise."

"I'll love him so much," Thad choked into her shoulder.

Erin closed her eyes against the tears flooding them. Today wasn't supposed to be about tears, but they were happy tears, at least. Hopefully the first of many more tears—and laughter—to come.

"We know you will," Carter assured Thad, his own voice gravelly. "We all will. Him *or* her."

Him or her. Yes, life had definitely changed, and as Erin cuddled Thad against her and told him all about what life would be like with a new baby, she knew she wouldn't have it any other way.

～

Did you enjoy **40 AND (SO OVER) FIXING IT**? If so, please consider leaving a review at your favorite online retailer to tell other readers about the book. And thank you!

For the latest on the next *SILVER FOXES OF BLACK WOLF'S BLUFF* release (and yes, there will be more!), be sure to sign up for my newsletter at ellasheridanauthor.com.

Before you go…

If you're enjoying the *SILVER FOXES OF BLACK WOLF'S BLUFF* series, be sure to check out Ella's *IF ONLY* series, where sexy contemporary meets unforgettable love and desire.

ONLY FOR THE WEEKEND

A blind date.
A fresh start.
Neither of them could've been more wrong.

It's been eight years since her best friend's brother rejected her. Jane Jacobs shouldn't still be thinking about him, fantasizing about him, comparing every man to him. It's time to take matters into her own hands—by going on a blind date with a Dom that won't remind her of the humiliating night she threw herself at V's feet. No, she'll be kneeling before someone else this time, for a weekend that will change everything.

Vincent O'Connell walked away from Jane years ago so he could become V, rock god of Weekend Washout, making panties drop and women scream. To drown out the chaos, he finds release in taking control completely, in the bedroom and out. Eight years ago he made a mistake he couldn't take back. Now, with Jane kneeling before him once again, walking away isn't an option. But to keep her, he'll have to tell her the truth, and that means revealing more than just his identity.

It means showing her his heart.

∽

"Scorching hot BDSM scenes and chemistry that's off the charts."

REVIEWS FROM THE HEART

∽

Looking for more unforgettable heroes and the women who love them? Try the men of the Enigma Team in Ella's *SOUTHERN NIGHTS: ENIGMA* series. Their lives are dangerous, and so is their love.

COME FOR ME

He lived a life of danger and loneliness without her. He's never going back.

• • •

Olivia Brannan never expected an ordinary workday to turn into a nightmare. She thought nothing could make her happier than having Dain as her husband. Her hard-core, intense alpha male. Protective to the extreme. Commanding—in and out of the bedroom. Her soul mate. They have everything they ever wanted. Or, almost everything. Until today.

Today, she found out she's pregnant. And unknowingly walked into a roomful of killers.

Ten years. That's how long Dain has lived his dream life. His wife is the partner he always wanted, in every way. And if they can't have children of their own, well, the elite team he runs at Atlanta's top security firm is often handful enough. They've created a "family" that fits them and fills their lives.

One phone call changes all that.

He never thought his wife could get pregnant. He never thought she'd be held hostage. Now it's up to him and his team to get the love of his life—and the child they never thought they'd have—out alive.

"Sizzles with heat from the first page!"

TBQ'S BOOK PALACE

About the Author

Ella Sheridan never fails to take her readers to the dark edges of love and back again. Strong heroines are her signature, and her heroes span the gamut from hot rock stars to alpha bodyguards and everywhere in between. Ella never pulls her punches, and her unique combination of raw emotion, hot sex, and action leave her readers panting for the next release.

Born and raised in the Deep South, Ella writes romantic suspense, erotic romance, and hot BDSM contemporaries. Start anywhere—every book may be read as a standalone, or begin with book one in any series and watch the ties between the characters grow.

Connect with Ella at her website, ellasheridanauthor.com, or at the social media options below. For news on Ella's new releases, free book opportunities, and more, sign up for Ella's newsletter. Or join Ella's Escape Room on Facebook for daily fun, games, and first dibs on all the news!

Made in the USA
Monee, IL
05 August 2023